Cross

The Ghost of Poplar Point

Also by Cynthia DeFelice

C YNTHIA D E F ELICE

The Ghost of Poplar Point

Farrar, Straus and Giroux / *New York*

To Enzo Koji DeFelice,
with love

The author gratefully acknowledges Dr. Wallace Chafe,
Research Professor of Linguistics at the University of California,
Santa Barbara, for sharing his knowledge of the
Seneca language and culture.

Copyright © 2007 by Cynthia C. DeFelice
All rights reserved
Distributed in Canada by Douglas & McIntyre Ltd.
Printed in the United States of America
Designed by Jay Colvin
First edition, 2007
1   3   5   7   9   10   8   6   4   2

www.fsgkidsbooks.com

Library of Congress Cataloging-in-Publication Data
DeFelice, Cynthia C.
    The ghost of Poplar Point / Cynthia DeFelice.— 1st ed.
      p.   cm.
    Summary: Prompted by the ghost of a young Seneca Indian girl, twelve-year-old Allie and her friend Dub are determined, despite the opposition of an unscrupulous property developer, that the historical pageant celebrating the founding of their town tell the truth about the fate of the Seneca people who lived there during the Revolutionary War.
    ISBN-13: 978-0-374-32540-4
    ISBN-10: 0-374-32540-5
    [1. Ghosts—Fiction.   2. Seneca Indians—Fiction.   3. Pageants—Fiction.
4. Indians of North America—New York (State)—Fiction.   5. New York (State)—Fiction]   I. Title.

PZ7.D3597 Gk 2007
[Fic]—dc22

                                                              2006047329

PRONUNCIATION GUIDE

Seneca vowels written with two dots over them (*ë* and *ö*) are nasalized, pronounced somewhat like the French vowels in *bien* and *bon*. A colon (:) shows that the preceding vowel is long (takes more time to pronounce). Seneca syllables may end with either *h* or a glottal stop (a catch in the throat), which is denoted with an apostrophe (').

Skayendady gyasonh (Sgayëdadih gya:söh) "My name is Skayendady."
Nyawenh (Nya:wëh) "Thank you."
Skennon (Sgë:nön') "Well-being, peace."
Ganondiyo (Ganödi:yo:h) Made-up name of a restored Seneca village.

Note that in all these words the second syllable is accented:

SkaYENdady (compare with the name of the New York city Schenectady)
gyaSONH
nyaWENH
skenNON
GaNONdiyo

The Ghost of Poplar Point

One

Allie Nichols sat in the third row of the old opera house, waiting her turn to audition for the starring role in the town's summer pageant. She had practiced her lines so often she almost knew them by heart, and knew just how she wanted to say them. But the longer she had to wait, the more nervous she became.

She watched as her friend Pam Wright stuttered and stammered her way through a bad case of stage fright. Next, another classmate of Allie's, Julie Horwitz, mumbled her lines quickly and in such a low voice that Allie doubted anyone in the auditorium could hear her.

Then a girl named Janelle Kavanaugh took the stage. From the whispers of the other kids, Allie learned that Janelle had moved to town just that year and that she went to a private school.

"Her mother's the one who wrote the script,"

Julie said in a low voice. "And I heard her dad gave all the money for it."

"Wow," said Pam. "He must be kind of a big shot, huh?"

Miss Lunsford, the pretty young director of the pageant, shot them a glance, and they stopped whispering as Janelle took a deep breath and cleared her throat. To their surprise, before she uttered one word, Janelle's face flushed an extraordinary shade of red and she fled from the stage in tears.

Next to try out was Karen Laver, a classmate who was well known to all the kids for her nasty remarks and mocking tongue. She read the entire speech loudly and, in Allie's opinion, rather overdramatically. But Karen received a polite round of applause for her performance.

"Okay, Allie, you're our final reader for this part," called Miss Lunsford.

Allie drew a deep breath and took the stage. She stood for a moment, squinting into the bright stage lights and trying to calm the fluttering in her stomach. She glanced at the audience and was immediately sorry. Karen, now sitting in the front row, was looking at her with a smug, challenging expression.

She told herself to ignore Karen and look instead at her best friend, Dub Whitwell, who sat one row behind Karen. Dub gave Allie a wide grin and a thumbs-up sign, and she tried to smile back.

Allie couldn't see a thing beyond the second row of seats, where Dub sat, and that was fine with her. The rest of the huge old theater loomed back there, dark and cavernous, and if she could see it, she undoubtedly would imagine it filled with people and be even more frightened than she already was.

"You may go ahead," Miss Lunsford said with an encouraging smile in Allie's direction.

Allie began without even looking at the paper in her hands. "Greetings, friends. My name is Laughs-like-a-waterfall. I am a Seneca Indian." *So far, so good,* she thought. Maybe this wasn't going to be so bad, after all.

Laughs-like-a-waterfall was the pageant's narrator. It was the most important role, with the most lines. Tryouts for the part were open to any girl in town who, like Allie, was twelve, or had just completed the sixth grade. The pageant, the town's first ever, was going to be the final event of the annual daylong summer festival on July 26. It was a depiction of the history of the town of Seneca, showing the relationship between the early European settlers and the local Seneca Indians.

"My age is twelve winters," Allie went on. Suddenly she felt a peculiar shivery sensation down her neck and across her shoulder blades. To her dismay, instead of the next line, she heard herself say, *"Skayendady gyasonh."*

5

The odd-sounding syllables echoed through the quiet hall. She felt her cheeks redden in embarrassment. Where had *that* come from?

There were muffled giggles from the audience. A few kids who hadn't been paying much attention before were now looking up at her with interest. One of the kids whispered loudly, "That wasn't in *my* script." Miss Lunsford shushed the crowd. In the silence, Allie coughed, then swallowed, and tried to collect herself before continuing.

"I belong to the Wolf Clan." *Whew,* she thought with relief. She was back on track.

But the next thing she said was another string of unintelligible words.

As the strange sounds fell from her lips, half of her brain screamed frantically, *Stop! What are you doing?*

The other half, recognizing all too well the odd, quivery feeling that was now running through her entire body, was thinking, *Oh, no, not again. Not now.*

She forced herself to go on, although she wasn't at all sure what would come out when she opened her mouth. "I wish to tell you a story. It is a story of how your people came to the lands of my people. It is a story of friendship." *Good,* she thought. *You're back to the script. Now finish quickly and get off the stage before you make even more of a fool of yourself.*

But then, unable to stop herself, she blurted another burst of incoherent sounds.

Allie watched as Dub's expression turned from puzzlement to concern. Karen Laver was holding a hand to her mouth, trying unsuccessfully to hide her delight at Allie's disaster.

Allie clamped her lips shut. Well, that was that. She'd never get the part now. She was about to flee the stage when she saw, to her surprise, that Miss Lunsford was smiling at her.

"Thank you, Allie. That was very interesting," Miss Lunsford said, standing and clapping. Slowly, uncertainly, others joined in the applause.

"Now, before we have the auditions for the role of Cornplanter, let's take a short break. You have five minutes, everyone, for a quick drink or trip to the bathroom." She held up her hand, fingers extended, and repeated, "*Five* minutes."

Allie rushed down the steps from the stage, anxious to talk to Dub about what had just happened, but she was blocked by the figure of Karen.

"Too bad, Allie," Karen said, her voice filled with mock sympathy. "You really blew it." Smiling then, she added, "Looks like I've got the part sewed up."

Allie wished for the perfect, witty retort to spring to her lips but, as always, she was too taken aback by Karen's nastiness to think.

Once, when Allie, in despair, had wondered why Karen was so mean, Pam had said it was because Karen was jealous.

"The other kids like you," Pam explained.

"They like Karen, too," Allie answered.

"No," said Pam, shaking her head. "They go along with her because they're afraid of her, not because they like her. Nobody wants to be her next victim."

Now, looking right into Karen's smirking face, Allie tried to follow Dub's often-repeated advice to ignore Karen Laver and everything she said. Sidestepping Karen, she headed toward Dub.

"Al, what happened up there?" he asked, looking worried.

"I'll tell you out in the lobby," Allie answered tersely.

When they were alone, Allie moaned, "Dub, I think it's happening again."

Dub looked quizzical. Then understanding dawned and his expression grew serious. "You mean . . . another *ghost*?"

To her surprise, in the past few months Allie had been visited by a series of three different ghosts. Each spirit had been unable to rest in peace because of an unresolved problem and had come to Allie for help. Each had finally been "put to rest," but only after Allie had taken action, sometimes at great risk to herself, to Dub, and, once, to her four-year-old brother, Michael.

Her sudden attraction for the unhappy spirits had

caused Dub to joke that she was a "ghost magnet." He was the only person who knew the whole story behind each of her otherworldly adventures, and she was very grateful to have him by her side. The discovery that ghosts not only existed but seemed determined to involve her in their affairs had been an unsettling one. It was fascinating and exhilarating, yes, but also frightening and dangerous.

Furthermore, she didn't really know why ghosts came to *her*. The question grew more puzzling when she discovered that her little brother, Michael, could see and hear the same spirits, though their parents had no idea that this was going on. That might not have worried Allie, except for one thing she and Dub had learned: ghosts were all different, just like the people they had once been. Some were kind, but some definitely were *not*.

Michael was too young to understand that some of the things he saw and heard were of supernatural origin, and as far as Allie was concerned the longer he remained in blissful ignorance, the better.

"Al? Hello? I asked you a question."

Dub's voice penetrated Allie's reverie. "Sorry," she said. "What did you say?"

"I *said*, was it a ghost who made you talk like that during the audition?"

Allie nodded. "It's the only explanation I can think of."

She had learned many of the ways ghosts could communicate and make their wishes known. Having someone else speak through her lips was just one of the interesting—and disconcerting—surprises she had experienced.

"At least the last time you came out with weird stuff you didn't mean to say, it was in English," Dub commented. "What was *that*?"

"I have no idea," Allie said. "And I can't believe Miss Lunsford was so nice, clapping and smiling afterward as if I'd done a great job. I mean, I totally blew it." She made a face, remembering Karen's comment. "Of course, Karen made sure to point that out to me."

Dub scowled and was about to answer when Miss Lunsford called loudly from the stage, "That's five minutes, people!"

"I'll stay for your audition, Dub," Allie said quickly. "But I'm going to sit in the back. That way, if I start babbling again, nobody will hear me."

Sitting alone in the dimly lit shadows at the rear of the old theater, Allie experienced a mixture of excitement and dread at the thought of another ghostly encounter. Whose spirit was trying to reach her this time, and what did it want from her?

Two

The next morning, Allie and Dub rode their bikes to the opera house and arrived about fifteen minutes early. Dub checked the door.

"It's open," he said to Allie, who was locking her bike to the rack. "We might as well go in."

They walked past the ticket booth and entered the shadowy lobby. The popcorn machine and drink dispenser glowed eerily in the lights from the red EXIT signs over the side doors, and the smell of popcorn filled the air. Allie always felt something special in the air of the old theater, and she decided it was excitement, the thrill of all the vaudeville shows, operas, and theatrical productions that had been performed here.

She and Dub were halfway across the lobby when they heard a man's voice coming from the stage area.

"We're here so my daughter can audition for the part of the narrator," he said.

Miss Lunsford's voice answered, sounding puzzled. "But she had her chance. Yesterday."

"Well, she wasn't ready yesterday," the man answered. "Today she is."

"Even so, Mr. Kavanaugh," said Miss Lunsford, "I'm sure you understand that it wouldn't be fair to the other children to give your daughter a second chance."

Allie and Dub crept to the open doorway and peered down the aisle. A man and a woman stood before Miss Lunsford, a girl behind them and to the side.

"It's Janelle—the girl who ran off the stage yesterday, crying," Allie whispered to Dub.

"She wants to try again?" Dub asked in surprise.

The man, Mr. Kavanaugh, was saying, "Janelle just had a bad day yesterday. You'll see. She'll do much better today." Turning to his daughter, he said, "Won't you, Janelle?"

Janelle said in a muffled voice, "I guess so."

"You're darned right you will. I told your mother to write the script with *you* in mind for the role of narrator. And since my company is sponsoring the pageant, I'm sure Miss Lunsford will be willing to give you a moment to show that you're ready to take on the part."

"But, Mr. Kavanaugh," Miss Lunsford said, "that really isn't fair to the other kids."

"I'll worry about what's fair, okay, miss?" Mr. Kavanaugh said shortly. "Janelle, why don't you sit down and run through your lines in your head while this lady and I have a little talk?"

Allie watched as Janelle walked over to the front row and took a seat. She looked at Dub with wide eyes when Miss Lunsford spoke again. "Mr. and Mrs. Kavanaugh, I'm sorry, but I've already chosen the girl who will play Laughs-like-a-waterfall. There are lots of other wonderful roles in this pageant, as you know. I'm sure Janelle will be perfect for one of them. She is welcome to stay this morning while we do the rest of the casting."

Allie poked Dub in the side and whispered, "Way to go, Miss Lunsford." She didn't know much about the director, except that she worked at the Chamber of Commerce and had volunteered to direct the pageant. But, watching her stand her ground with Mr. Kavanaugh, Allie had to admire the woman's spunk.

Mr. and Mrs. Kavanaugh looked at each other. Mrs. Kavanaugh said, "Darryl, there *are* other good parts that would be fine for Janelle—"

But Mr. Kavanaugh interrupted his wife and said angrily to Miss Lunsford, "Are you saying you refuse to give my daughter a second chance?"

"I—" Miss Lunsford began, sounding flustered. "I really don't think it would be—"

Mr. Kavanaugh added before she could finish, "I know, fair to the other kids. So you said." He smiled, and his voice changed, becoming chummy and confidential. "But you haven't announced yet who the narrator will be, have you?"

Miss Lunsford shook her head.

"So no one will even know there's been a change," Mr. Kavanaugh said heartily, raising his hands and his shoulders in an exaggerated shrug. "Nothing unfair about that." Turning to Janelle, he said, "Go ahead, honey. Get up there and show this lady what a good narrator you'll be."

Janelle stood still as her mother said hesitantly, "Darryl, maybe—"

Mr. Kavanaugh interrupted her again to say, "Go on, Janelle."

"Mr. Kavanaugh," said Miss Lunsford, "I really can't allow this."

There was silence for a moment before Mr. Kavanaugh spoke in a low voice. "Then you might want to ask yourself this: would it be *fair* to the other kids to cancel the entire pageant over a misunderstanding about this one little part?"

Miss Lunsford looked puzzled for a moment; then her expression darkened.

Mr. Kavanaugh sighed. "Let's be reasonable here. I could go to the town council and to the head of the Chamber of Commerce—who is, I believe, your boss—and see what they have to say. Of course, I'd rather not involve them when we could resolve this issue very easily right now, with no one being the wiser. But if you force me . . ." His voice trailed off, and he looked at Miss Lunsford and waited.

After a moment's silence, Miss Lunsford said, "Go to them, then, if that's the way you wish to handle this. I hope they won't agree to cancel the pageant. That would be very disappointing." She turned to Janelle and added softly, "The rest of the children will be here for about an hour or so this morning. We'll be making the remaining casting decisions. If you'd like to stay and try out for a part other than narrator, we'd be happy to have you."

Janelle looked at her father. "Dad? Should I?"

"No. We're leaving," her father said tightly. To Miss Lunsford he said, "I'm going to get this thing straightened out right now."

Quickly Allie and Dub moved away from the doorway and pretended to be just entering the theater as Mr. and Mrs. Kavanaugh came through the lobby and went out the front entrance with Janelle at their heels. Allie looked curiously at the girl to see if Janelle was mortified by her father's behavior. Allie certainly would have been if her father ever acted like that. But the other girl's eyes were downcast, and Allie couldn't read anything from her face.

"*Man,*" said Dub when the door had closed behind them. "*That* was interesting." Then he wiggled his eyebrows and said mysteriously, "Now only one question remains . . ."

"What?" asked Allie.

"Who is the girl who *did* get the part?"

Three

Allie followed Dub down the aisle and they took seats in the front row. Soon other kids began to show up, including Julie Horwitz and Pam Wright, who both looked glum. Karen Laver arrived, wearing her dark hair in two long braids topped off with a beaded headband.

"Gee, you wouldn't be trying to influence Miss Lunsford's decision by wearing that Indian maiden getup, would you, Karen?" asked Dub.

"I'm only trying to show her that I can look the part," Karen retorted.

"You look the part, all right," Dub answered. Under his breath he added, "The part of a suck-up."

"What did you say?" Karen demanded.

"Nothing," answered Dub innocently. "I was just wishing you luck."

Karen made a face at Dub and turned away, crossing her arms over her chest.

Julie whispered to Allie, "I hope you get to be narrator. I know it won't be me."

"Well, it sure won't be me," said Pam. "I'm glad, actually, after what happened yesterday. If I was that nervous in tryouts, can you picture me in the real pageant? I'd probably faint or throw up in front of the whole town."

Brad Lewis said, "Being a stagehand is the way to go, right, Joey?"

"For sure," Joey Fratto agreed. "No lines to memorize, no worries about screwing up in public."

"Well, you two can have that behind-the-scenes stuff," Karen announced. "Personally, if I don't get the main part, I'm out of here. No way I'm going to waste my time on some bit part."

"That's what we love about you, Karen," said Dub with a cheerful smile. "Your good sportsmanship is an inspiration to us all."

"As if I care what you think, Dub Whitwell," Karen replied scornfully.

Miss Lunsford called for order and began reading the list of cast members. Allie, Pam, Julie, Joey, and Brad all cheered when she said that Dub had been chosen to play the famous Seneca orator Cornplanter.

"And Allie Nichols will have the part of Laughs-like-a-waterfall," Miss Lunsford announced.

Allie's mouth fell open in astonishment. Her friends clapped, and Dub turned to give her a high five. Karen muttered angrily to Allie, "You must have brownnosed Miss Lunsford like you did Mr. Henry. You were his little pet all year, and now this. I totally can't believe it."

Allie was too surprised to respond. It was useless to try to explain to Karen that she hadn't done anything to become Mr. Henry's "pet." He was her favorite teacher in the world, and she couldn't help it if he liked her, too. As far as she could tell, he liked all the kids, even Karen.

Miss Lunsford went on, addressing Allie directly. "I thought it was very creative of you to add those authentic Seneca Indian words to your speech."

Authentic Seneca Indian words? "Ummmm . . ." Allie said, hesitating. After a lengthy pause, she saw Dub looking at her and mouthing the words *Say something.*

"Well, I'm not exactly sure those were real Indian words, but I was thinking it would be more"—her voice trailed off as she tried to remember the word Miss Lunsford had used—"authentic if we *did* add some."

"I agree," Miss Lunsford said enthusiastically. "That's very creative thinking. Come to me after today's rehearsal, please, and we'll talk about it." She turned to Karen, who was raising her hand. "Yes?"

"I've got to go," Karen said. "I only came today to tell you that I can't be in the pageant. I just have too many other things to do this summer."

Miss Lunsford looked puzzled for a moment. Then she said, "I see. Very well, Karen. You may be excused."

Karen got up to leave. In a voice just low enough so Miss Lunsford couldn't hear, she said, "What a relief. Now I won't have to waste my vacation hanging around with you losers."

"We'll try our best to get over our disappointment," said Dub.

When Karen had gone, Julie grinned. "Well, I'm over it," she said. "How about you guys?"

They all laughed. Allie glanced at Pam and was relieved to see that she was laughing, too. For a long time, Pam had been under Karen's thumb, too scared to do anything except what Karen wanted her to do. But recently, after getting to know Allie and Dub better, Pam had realized that she preferred to hang out with them. This had only made Karen's attacks on Allie and Dub nastier than ever.

Allie and the other kids returned their attention to Miss Lunsford. As she went through all the parts, kids signed up to be either settlers or Indians or, in some cases, backstage workers or scenery painters. Janelle did not appear; neither did her parents.

"Now," said Miss Lunsford, "we're going to need

help with props and costumes. I may be asking you to bring things in from home. But I've had a generous offer from a local businessman who believes he'll be able to supply most of what we need."

"It's my Uncle Hal," Brad called out proudly.

Miss Lunsford looked confused. "*Your* Uncle Hal?" she asked.

"Yeah," Brad answered. "I know, it's weird because his store is called Uncle Hal's, and everybody calls him that. But he's my for-real uncle."

"He's the guy you interviewed for the assignment Mr. Henry gave us, right?" asked Joey. "The one who wins burping contests and smashes beer cans on his forehead?"

"Yeah," said Brad proudly. "Only now he's into kung fu. He's working on something called the Iron Palm. He already broke a board in half with his bare hand! His goal is to break three cinder blocks."

"Wow," said Joey. "I'd like to see that!"

"People," Miss Lunsford said loudly, in an effort to reclaim their attention. "As I said, Uncle Hal— Brad's uncle—has offered to help, and he's going to come to a rehearsal this week to get you all fitted in costumes. Meanwhile, I'd like you to study your scripts tonight and be ready for a run-through in the morning. Thank you, everyone. You are dismissed until tomorrow at ten o'clock."

Allie asked Dub to wait for her, and after the

other kids had gone, she approached Miss Lunsford.

"So, Allie," Miss Lunsford said, "if those phrases you spoke weren't in the Seneca language, where did they come from?"

Allie imagined herself explaining to Miss Lunsford that a ghost had taken over her mouth and made her speak a bunch of nonsense words. It was impossible. "I just sort of made them up," she said, regretting the way being a ghost magnet caused her to lie.

"Well, I think adding the language was a brilliant idea. That's *improvising*, as we say in the theater," Miss Lunsford said with a smile. "I'm hoping to encourage improvisation in this production. It makes things so much more interesting. But to make the idea work, we need to find some *real* Seneca words for you to use."

"I—well, I'll try," Allie said.

"Good," Miss Lunsford said. "With all the Seneca Indian history around this area, I'm sure we'll be able to find someone who can help us. Come to think of it, there's a restored Seneca village called Ganondiyo not far from here. Have you ever heard of it?"

Allie thought for a moment. "It sounds kind of familiar," she said.

"I think there are people there who speak Seneca. Let's look into it," said Miss Lunsford. "In the meantime, you study your lines as they were written. We'll make adjustments later if we can. Okay?"

"Sure," said Allie. "And thanks for giving me the part."

Miss Lunsford smiled at her warmly. "I didn't give it to you, Allie. You earned it. I know you'll bring something special to this role."

Allie wanted to ask if there was going to be trouble with Mr. Kavanaugh, but she couldn't let on that she and Dub had been listening. She turned quickly to escape. Before she could get away, though, she answered Miss Lunsford by saying, *"Nyawenh."*

Whatever that means, she thought. With an embarrassed grin, she fled the room.

Dub was waiting for her on the street outside the opera house. "What did she want?" he asked.

"She wants me to see if I can find some real Indian words to use in the pageant." Allie paused and added, "I answered her in that crazy talk."

"Mmmm," said Dub. "Something is definitely up with that." Then he suggested, "We can search Indian words on the Internet." His parents had just opened a computer store in town, and Dub was always up on the latest technology.

"You'll help me, then?" Allie asked. "I don't mean only with the Internet stuff, either." She gave Dub a pleading look. "If this is another ghost . . ." Her voice trailed off.

"Are you kidding?" said Dub. "If this is another

ghost, do you think I'm going to miss out on all the action?"

Allie gave a sigh of relief.

Dub went on. "I mean, think about it. If I didn't hang around with you, I'd never have the opportunity to get scared out of my wits, risk my life, *and* get in trouble with my parents and the police, all at the same time."

"Dub!" Allie cried, laughing. But, really, everything he'd said was true. She and Dub *had* been grounded for a week after their last experience with a ghost, and there *had* been some terrifying moments and, okay, there *had* been a police officer or two involved. "It worked out in the end," she said lamely.

"True," Dub agreed. "So far, so good. Anyway, whatever happens next, I'm in."

Allie smiled. Good old Dub, computer wizard and true-blue friend.

"So what do you want to do now?" Dub asked.

"That question," said Allie with a happy sigh, "is the single best thing about summer vacation. We have all the time in the world."

"Good thing," Dub said. "Because it looks like *ghosts* don't take vacations."

Four

"I got the part," Allie announced that night at the dinner table.

"That's terrific, Allie-Cat," said her father, while her mother beamed at her proudly.

Looking at her parents' kind faces, she was tempted to add that she had babbled nonsense words during her audition, and that she was pretty sure another ghost had shown up. Her parents loved her, and they always tried to understand her. But they worried about her, too, especially about what they sometimes called her "overactive imagination." At one point, they had even talked of having her "see someone" about it, which Allie knew meant going to a shrink.

She'd never be able to explain—not to her mom and dad and especially not to a doctor—everything that had been happening for the past few months. The more time that went by, the harder it became to announce to her parents and the rest of the world, "Hey, guess what? Ghosts are real, and I can hear them and see them!"

Thank goodness for Dub, she thought, or she'd worry that she and Michael were both crazy.

"It's the main speaking part, right?" asked her mother.

Allie nodded.

"What's your Indian name again?" asked her father.

"Laughs-like-a-waterfall," Allie answered.

Michael was looking at her with a puzzled frown. "That's dumb," he said. "Waterfalls don't laugh."

"You know, you're right, Mike," said Allie. "The lady who wrote the script must have thought it sounded pretty, or something."

"Well, it's dumb," Michael repeated matter-of-factly.

"I wonder if it's a real Indian name," said Allie. "Anyway, we *are* going to add some Indian words to the script."

"That would be a nice touch," said Mrs. Nichols. Then she sighed and said, "I should bake something for the shindig at the store tomorrow, but I'm so tired from cleaning and making new displays, I don't think I can face it."

Mrs. Nichols ran an antiques store in town, and Allie loved to help out. "Do you want me to make cookies?" she asked. "You promised refreshments in the newspaper ad."

"Thanks, honey, but you need to study your script. I'll just buy some cookies at the Sweet Shop on my way in tomorrow." She sighed again and said to Mr. Nichols, "I hope Darryl's plan for boosting business downtown pays off. It was his idea for every store to have a big sale on the same day."

Darryl, Allie thought. Where had she just heard that name? Then she remembered Janelle Kavanaugh's father. "Mom, is your new landlord Darryl Kavanaugh?"

"Yes. Why?"

"He was at the theater today. He's kind of a jerk, and so is his daughter, Janelle."

"Allie!" her mother protested. "Why would you say that?"

Allie told about overhearing Mr. Kavanaugh's discussion with Miss Lunsford. She added, "And Janelle went right along with it. She didn't care about being fair."

Mrs. Nichols looked surprised, then troubled. "I don't like the sound of that at all," she said. "I guess I don't know much about Darryl, other than that he's a better landlord than I had before. I do appreciate the way he fixed the plumbing, painted, and put in those new windows."

"He's made improvements on a lot of other buildings downtown, too," Mr. Nichols said. "There was an article in the paper about him the other day. The headline called him the 'Town Hero.' "

Allie noticed that Michael had been quietly marching his favorite Galactic Warrior through a puddle of ketchup on his plate. He held up the dripping action figure and announced, "Moray Eel-Man's a *real* hero! Look, he's all covered in blood, and he's not even scared."

"Michael, you know you're not supposed to play with toys at the table!" Mrs. Nichols cried. She leaped up to get a dishcloth and wiped Michael's hands and Moray Eel-Man's feet.

When they'd finished eating and Allie had cleared the table, she went to her room and climbed onto the bed with the script to study her lines. " 'My people lived on Seneca Lake at the place now known as Poplar Point, where the creek enters the lake from Fossil Glen,' " she read aloud. " 'There we grew corn, beans, and squash for our food. These we called the Three Sisters. Also, we had orchards where we grew apples and peaches. We kept hogs and chickens.' "

Allie tried to add a dramatic flair to the stiff words that Mrs. Kavanaugh had written. She couldn't help wishing they didn't sound as if they'd been copied from her social studies book.

It was hard to keep her mind from wandering,

and she struggled to focus. But she must have fallen asleep because some time later she awoke, startled and disturbed, from an awful nightmare. It was filled with the sounds of gunshots and screams of fear and cries of pain. Panicked people were running in all directions. The air was thick with either mist or smoke, so Allie wasn't able to make out who was shooting at whom. She lay on top of the covers, her pulse racing, trying to shake the terrible dread and confusion brought on by the dream.

There had been something familiar in the scene, something she recognized. But it was fading, even as her mind tried to grasp what it had been.

That she had had such a dream did not surprise her. Each ghost she'd encountered so far had communicated with her through dreams. Was this nightmare a message from her new ghost? If so— *Oh, no!* She had learned, to her dismay, that when she was contacted by a ghost through a dream, Michael had the same dream. Was Michael now waking from the nightmare as she had, alone and scared in his bed?

She jumped up and ran down the hallway to Michael's room. His bed was empty. Her heart sank. *Where was he?* Quickly she scanned the room. The large glowing face of Michael's Galactic Warriors digital clock showed ten minutes past eight. Relieved, Allie realized that while she had dozed off over her script, Michael hadn't even gone to bed yet. He hadn't experienced the nightmare, since he'd been awake at the time.

So far, Allie had been able to protect Michael from the worst of the fear and danger that came from being a ghost magnet. She told herself that with Dub at her side, she could handle whatever situations might arise. After all, she and Dub were twelve. But Mike was only four, and far more vulnerable. She wasn't sure how long she'd be able to keep him safe, and that added greatly to her anxiety about having another visit from a ghost.

She had been lucky today, and so had Mike. But what, she wondered, about the next time?

Five

The next morning, Allie and Michael ate cereal as their mother squeezed fresh lemons into a pitcher. "Allie," she said, "do you think you could stop by the store after your rehearsal? If we're mobbed, I might need help."

"Sure," said Allie. "Dub'll probably be with me. Is it okay if he comes?"

"Of course. Now will you go up with Mike and get his teeth brushed, please? Your father will be ready to leave soon."

"I don't want to go to Fritzi's today," declared Michael. "I want to help at the store, too."

Fritzi was Michael's baby-sitter. Ordinarily he loved going to her house, and looked forward to it so eagerly that Mrs. Nichols claimed to be jealous.

Allie saw the stubborn set of Michael's chin that sometimes meant big trouble was coming. She knew her mother had no time that morning for one of his rare but spectacular tantrums, so she tried to think of a way to distract him.

"Aww, Mom," she said, "on second thought, do I *have* to go to the store today? It'll be so boring. And Dub and I were going to do something really fun, like"—she glanced at Michael—"going to the water park."

"I go to the water park with Fritzi!" Michael said excitedly. "I stomp on all the squirts, like this!" He jumped up from the table and demonstrated how he stepped on each one of the jets of water that came up from the ground at the park.

"Like this—and this—and *this*!" Michael went on, stomping on each blue tile on the kitchen floor.

"Is that what you're going to do today?" Allie asked innocently.

"Yes! Fritzi said."

"Well, you're a lucky duck," said Allie, pretending to pout. "I have to work at the boring old store."

"I'm a lucky duck," Michael sang happily.

"Come on, lucky duck, let's go brush our teeth," suggested Allie.

Leading Michael from the kitchen, she looked back at her mother, who smiled at her and mouthed the words *Nice work*.

After Michael had left happily with his dad for Fritzi's house, Allie said goodbye to her mother and rode her bike to Dub's. Side by side, they pedaled slowly downtown to the opera house for the first day of actual rehearsal.

"Do you know your lines?" Allie asked.

"I sound pretty good in my room in front of the mirror," Dub answered with a grin. "But there's no telling what'll happen onstage. That old theater is so big; it kind of freaks me out to look out at all the rows and rows of seats. Not to mention the balconies."

"When I was little, I wouldn't go up in the balconies," said Allie. "I thought they were haunted." She laughed and added, "And that was before I knew any *real* ghosts."

"Speaking of ghosts, any new developments?" Dub asked.

Allie told him about her nightmare, and her worries about Michael having bad dreams along with her. "I'm afraid to go to sleep because I don't want Mike to be scared."

"Well, let's hope we find out something soon," said Dub. "You can't exactly stay awake twenty-four hours a day."

As usual, Dub's understanding and sympathy made Allie feel better.

Approaching the main part of town, they had to ride single file and watch for traffic. Allie pulled ahead of Dub and they went the rest of the way without talking.

When they reached the theater, they saw a van parked out front with the rear doors flung open. The van was painted in a camouflage pattern. On the side, in large, bright red letters, was written UNCLE HAL'S ARMY SURPLUS AND RENT-A-CENTER—IF UNCLE HAL DOESN'T HAVE IT, YOU DON'T NEED IT! A life-size replica of a bald eagle, wings spread and talons outstretched, was mounted on the roof.

At that moment, a man came out of the theater and walked toward them. Allie saw that he matched the van: he was dressed in camouflage pants, boots, and shirt. The shirt's sleeves were rolled up above his biceps, and as he came closer Allie could see a tattoo on one arm. She smiled when she realized it was Bugs Bunny, holding a carrot, with a word balloon that read, "What's up, Doc?"

The man, obviously Uncle Hal himself, reached into the driver's-side window of the van. A loud horn blared a raucous "A-OOO-GA" sound, making Allie and Dub both jump. The man grinned. "Hi, kids."

"Hi," Allie and Dub said together.

"Can you really smash a beer can on your forehead?" Dub asked.

Uncle Hal's grin grew wider. "Has that nephew of mine been bragging on his Uncle Hal?"

"He told our whole class about you," Allie said.

"And about the burping contests," Dub added.

"Well, it's true, I have won a few in my time, and

I have the trophies to prove it," Uncle Hal said modestly. "But don't you go trying that business with the cans, you hear? Leave it to the professionals."

"Okay," said Dub with a laugh. "But Brad said you're into kung fu now."

Uncle Hal let out a sharp, explosive breath and moved suddenly, landing in a graceful pose with his arms raised and his knees bent. Then he straightened, let his arms fall, and said solemnly, "As disciples, we strive to be wise and calm and to cultivate self-control. But if we are set upon by an enemy, we fight like all get-out."

"Can you break a cinder block with your hands yet?" Dub asked eagerly.

"So far, all I've got is one broken board and a broken hand," Uncle Hal admitted. He roared with laughter, adding, "It's plenty sore, anyhow."

Just then Karen Laver passed by, pedaling very slowly on her bike and gazing at them disdainfully. She drawled, "I am *so* glad I got out of that stupid pageant when I did."

"Why don't you mind your own business, Karen?" said Dub.

"But you *are* my business," Karen said sweetly. "I like to keep up on what the town's two biggest losers are doing. It's so entertaining." She wiggled her fingers as she passed by. "Tootles."

"Tootles to you, too," Allie muttered.

"Whew," said Uncle Hal with a low whistle, "what's eating her?"

"Oh, she's always like that," Dub said.

Uncle Hal shook his head. "People sure find strange ways to enjoy themselves," he said.

Allie smiled to herself at this remark, coming as it did from a man with Uncle Hal's hobbies.

"So you kids are in the pageant," Uncle Hal said. "How about helping me carry this stuff in?"

"Sure."

Uncle Hal was rummaging in the rear of the van when Brad Lewis rode up on his bike. "Hey, Uncle Hal!" he called.

"Hey, little buddy!"

Brad and Uncle Hal exchanged high fives. Then Uncle Hal handed a large cardboard box to each of the kids, grabbed two more, and nudged the van doors shut with his elbow. "Looks like that'll do it," he said. He winked and added, "Let's take these in to that cute young lady who's running the show."

When they had delivered the boxes and the rest of the kids had shown up, Miss Lunsford called for order. "I'd like you all to meet Mr. Lewis," she began.

"Uncle Hal's fine, ma'am," Uncle Hal interjected. "Or just plain Hal, if you like." He gave her a big smile. "You say 'Mr. Lewis,' I think you're talking about my dad."

"All right, then," Miss Lunsford agreed. She

smiled back at him and added, "But you'll have to drop the 'ma'am,' or I'll think you're talking about my mother."

Uncle Hal laughed. "So I should call you . . . ?"

Allie watched as a blush rose to Miss Lunsford's cheeks. "Beth will be fine."

Dub nudged Allie and whispered, "Go, Uncle Hal!"

Miss Lunsford cleared her throat and turned back to the cast. "So, as I was saying, Uncle Hal has generously offered to supply us with props and costumes for the play. Those of you who are settlers, please see me. Indians, please go over to the other side of the stage with Uncle Hal. Technicians and scenery people, Uncle Hal put some boxes backstage for you. Look through them carefully, and take what you think will be useful."

A flurry of activity followed while the settlers tried on old-fashioned dresses, bonnets, hats, and pants with suspenders, and the Indians donned clothing made of a material that the kids agreed looked like real buckskin. In less than an hour they were all outfitted, and had stowed their costumes in plastic bags labeled with their names. Allie loved the special beaded headpiece she would wear as Laughs-like-a-waterfall.

Brad, Joey, and the other stagehands proudly showed the frames they had assembled for hanging the scenery. Some of the boys carried on a mock battle using the muskets and bows and arrows Uncle Hal had provided, until Miss Lunsford flashed the lights on and off to restore order.

"We'll take a five-minute break now, people," she announced. "Then we'll regroup and go through the opening scene. First, though, let's give a big thank-you to Uncle Hal for his help."

"Thanks, Uncle Hal," the kids chorused.

"No problem," Uncle Hal answered. With a little wink at Miss Lunsford, he turned to leave. Brad and Dub and some of the other kids started to accompany him up the aisle. Allie was about to follow when Miss Lunsford approached her. The director's face, so happy just a moment before, now appeared tense. "Allie, I need to speak with you."

"Oh," said Allie, surprised. "Sure."

"Let's go where we can have some privacy," Miss Lunsford said, heading to a little room backstage.

Curious and a bit uneasy now, Allie went with her.

Miss Lunsford took a deep breath and said tightly, "I'm afraid I have some bad news." She paused, and a muscle in her jaw jumped. "I've had to make a casting change. You won't be playing Laughs-like-a-waterfall, after all."

Allie blinked.

Miss Lunsford went on quickly. "I'm sorry, Allie. I got a call last night from the head of the town council, and another from my boss at the Chamber of Commerce. What it boiled down to was that if another girl didn't get the part, the pageant was going to be canceled. I had to make a decision between letting down one person—you—and disappointing the entire town."

"But that isn't—"

"It isn't fair, I know." Miss Lunsford reached out and squeezed one of Allie's hands in hers. "This is not the way I like to do things."

Allie remembered the scene she'd witnessed the morning before. "Janelle Kavanaugh's getting the part, isn't she?" she asked.

Miss Lunsford nodded. "How did you know?"

Not really wanting to admit that she and Dub had been eavesdropping, even if it had been by mistake, Allie said, "I—I heard her father is giving the money for the pageant."

Miss Lunsford nodded again, her lips tight. "It's the worst kind of small-town dirty dealings—" She broke off and looked away for a moment. Then she repeated, "I'm sorry, Allie. I'm afraid you'll have to give the beaded headpiece to Janelle, and you'll play one of the Indian girls. But I think we can still incorporate your idea of speaking in Seneca. How does that sound?"

Allie was still too surprised and disappointed to answer. She shrugged.

Miss Lunsford nodded sympathetically. "I don't blame you for being upset. If it helps, I suspect Janelle feels terrible about this. She couldn't have wanted to get the part this way."

"Then she should have said so," Allie muttered.

Miss Lunsford sighed. "Her father was very insistent. I hope you won't hold it against her."

Allie didn't answer, and the director appeared to take her silence as agreement.

Miss Lunsford smiled ruefully. "I appreciate your understanding, Allie." She patted Allie's shoulder and walked out of the small room.

Allie stood where she was, feeling tears spring to her eyes. Glad no one was there to see, she brushed them away.

Returning to the auditorium, she took a seat near the side wall and tried to get a grip on her emotions. Janelle had stolen the part that was rightfully hers, and Allie *did* hold it against her, no matter what Miss Lunsford had said. Janelle should have spoken up and said she didn't want the part. Why hadn't she? It was what Allie would have done.

Along with her anger and disappointment, she felt the distinctive prickly feeling that meant her ghost was present.

Uh-oh, she thought. *What now?*

Six

When the other kids returned, Allie looked at Dub. He looked questioningly back at her, obviously wondering why she was sitting alone at the end of the fourth row. He started over toward her, but Miss Lunsford told everyone to quiet down and take their seats. "In the scenes where the settlers and Indians first meet and get together for a feast, there are many of you who don't have lines to speak," she said. "You'll be onstage, though, and I don't want you to simply stand around like part of the scenery. You should pretend to talk to one another, stir the cooking pots, act busy doing the things that you think would be going on. I'm not going to tell you specifically what to do; just improvise.

"Okay, now let's begin with Laughs-like-a-waterfall's opening speech. There has been a casting change in this role. Janelle, take your place, please.

Allie, for now you come on up and join the others who are improvising."

Several kids, including Dub, turned in their seats to stare at Allie with surprise. When she saw the shock and sympathy in Dub's eyes, she quickly looked down, afraid she might cry again.

She stood onstage and listened in disbelief as Janelle stammered and stuttered through her lines. As Janelle was trying for the fourth time to get through her introductory speech, Allie felt a familiar stirring inside. Suddenly she called out loudly and insistently, *"Skayendady gyasonh!"*

Some of the kids laughed, and others looked at her as if she'd gone crazy. Miss Lunsford turned to her with a puzzled expression and said softly, "That is not quite the kind of improvisation I'm looking for, Allie."

But when Janelle resumed her speech, Allie found herself blurting out several more strange sentences.

"Allie, since you can't control yourself, I'm afraid I have to ask you to leave," Miss Lunsford said unhappily. "Come back tomorrow with a better attitude, please."

Allie left the stage and walked in a daze up the aisle and out into the glare of the morning sun, unable to believe what was happening to her. Not knowing what else to do with herself, and needing to talk to Dub, she waited by the bike rack for him to come out.

"It is so unfair, I can't believe it!" Allie shouted to him when he appeared. As they rode their bikes slowly down the back alley behind the opera house, she shared the whole story. "Janelle should have told her father she didn't want to be in the pageant. Or she could have said she wanted a different part. A part that wasn't already taken!"

Dub nodded sympathetically. "Especially since she *still* can't say her lines without stammering all over the place!"

Allie cried, "She was awful!"

"She was so bad I actually felt kind of sorry for her," Dub said.

"Whose side are you on, anyway?" Allie asked testily.

"Al, come on," Dub answered. "You know I'm on your side. I'm just saying Janelle didn't exactly look like she was having the time of her life up there. She had to be embarrassed. *I* sure would have been."

"Then she should have admitted she's no good for the part and stepped down," said Allie grumpily. "Instead, I got yelled at about my *attitude*! I couldn't help saying those things!"

"*I* know that, Al," said Dub. "But nobody else does, including Miss Lunsford. She's got to think you're acting like a sore loser."

Allie sighed. She had no reason to yell at Dub. He was only trying to help. And he was right. "I can't very well tell Miss Lunsford the truth," she said wearily. "So what *can* I say? I should just drop out of the pageant altogether."

"That's not the answer," said Dub. "And, anyway," he added quietly, "you might not be able to quit."

"What do you mean?" Allie demanded.

"In case you haven't noticed, this latest ghost of yours seems to be very interested in the pageant."

"So?" Allie said cautiously.

"Well, if the reason the ghost came to you has something to do with the pageant, it may not let you quit."

May not let you.

The phrase echoed in Allie's head as they pedaled in silence the rest of the way to Mrs. Nichols's antiques shop.

Seven

"Wow," said Allie as she and Dub entered her mother's shop. "I've never seen this place so crowded."

Mrs. Nichols, her face flushed and happy, looked up and waved from the other side of the store, where she was taping bubble wrap around a china vase.

Dub and Allie went over, and Mrs. Nichols exclaimed, "Boy, am I glad to see you two! We've been busier than I ever expected. Reggie's out back loading a dresser into Leslie Buell's van. Would you mind refilling the cookie tray and putting out more napkins? Also, could you check the lemonade pitcher?"

"Okay, Mom," said Allie. She wanted to tell her mother about what had happened at rehearsal, but she could see it wasn't the right time.

"I'll get the cookies," said Dub. "But I should probably do a taste test, don't you think? Just to make sure they haven't gone stale or anything."

"Good idea, Dub," said Mrs. Nichols with a laugh. "I can always count on you." She turned to Allie. "After you get the refreshments squared away, would you and Dub mind the front desk while I stay out on the floor and help customers?"

"Sure!" Allie said. She loved ringing up sales on the cash register, taking people's credit cards, checks, and cash, and making change.

After the food table was restocked, she and Dub took their positions behind the front desk, munching on white chocolate chip cookies. Allie noticed that the cookies appeared to be meeting with Dub's full approval.

She was showing Dub how to run a credit card through the scanner when she heard a voice that sounded vaguely familiar. She looked up and was amazed to see that Mr. and Mrs. Kavanaugh had entered the store, followed by Janelle. Allie nudged Dub, rolled her eyes, and said, "Look who's here."

Dub's eyebrows lifted.

Janelle hadn't noticed them yet. She positioned herself behind a large wooden coatrack, as if trying to make herself invisible, or at least as inconspicuous as possible.

Mrs. Nichols said, "Why, hello, Eileen. Hi, Darryl."

"Can you believe it?" Allie muttered to Dub. "That creep is my mom's new landlord."

Dub muttered back, "Then he's my parents' land-lord, too. I never knew his name before."

"I think he owns the whole town," Allie said darkly.

"Business is booming," Mr. Kavanaugh said in a loud, hearty voice. "That's what we like to see."

"Today has been absolutely crazy," Mrs. Nichols said brightly, pushing back a stray lock of hair from her forehead. "This town-wide sale idea of yours was a good one, Darryl. I had a minute to talk with some of the other shop owners, and everyone's having a fantastic day."

Mr. Kavanaugh smiled. "The sale is just the beginning. I have big plans for this town, Ann."

Mrs. Nichols said, "Darryl and Eileen, I don't believe you know my daughter, Allie, and her friend Dub Whitwell." She gestured toward the desk. "They're here helping out today. Allie and Dub, I'd like you to meet Mr. and Mrs. Kavanaugh."

After everyone had said their hellos, Mr. Kavanaugh turned to Dub. "Whitwell, eh? Your parents run the computer store, right?"

"Yes," said Dub.

"How do you like the improvements I made to the place? Looks great, don't you think?"

Dub gave a little nod, but didn't say anything. Allie knew how he felt: there was no need to praise Mr. Kavanaugh when he was doing such a good job of it himself.

Mr. Kavanaugh looked around irritably and called, "Janelle?" To his wife he said, "Where is she?" He called again, "Janelle? Are you hiding?"

Janelle came out from behind the coatrack. She glanced toward Allie, and her face flushed a deep, blotchy red. Their eyes locked for several long seconds, and then Janelle's mother urged her forward and introduced her. After the introductions, Janelle bent her head to stare fixedly at her feet. She didn't let on that she'd ever seen Allie and Dub before, and they didn't show it, either.

Allie still hadn't had a chance to tell her mother about losing her part to Janelle, and she doubted that the Kavanaughs knew she was the girl Janelle had replaced. An awkward silence hung over the group.

Mrs. Nichols broke it by saying, "Allie and Dub both have parts in the pageant. I understand you wrote the script, Eileen."

"Oh, it was Darryl's idea, really," said Mrs. Kavanaugh with a modest little shrug.

"I wanted to add something new and special to the festival this year," Mr. Kavanaugh said. "I thought the pageant would help to build pride in the town. It's kind of a tie-in to the hotel and conference center my company is building out on the lake at Poplar Point. Actually, that's the reason we're here."

"Oh?" said Mrs. Nichols.

"Yes," said Mr. Kavanaugh. "We were wondering if you have any Indian relics for sale."

Mrs. Nichols frowned. "I'm not sure exactly what you mean. What kinds of things are you looking for?"

Mrs. Kavanaugh said, "Well, we were thinking of war bonnets, bows and arrows, tomahawks . . ."

Allie's mother looked puzzled, and Mr. Kavanaugh broke in. "See, I thought it would be terrific to draw on our local history and follow an Indian theme in the decor of the place. That would make it really unique, don't you think?"

Allie noticed that he didn't bother to wait for an answer but continued, "We need some stuff to give the place atmosphere. I was thinking of setting up a tepee in the lobby, that kind of thing. And I'd like to decorate the walls of the restaurant with Indian-style tools and trinkets."

Mrs. Nichols said, "Oh, I see."

Allie could tell that her mother was feeling uncomfortable, and she knew why.

Mrs. Nichols went on, "Of course, the Senecas lived in longhouses, not tepees. Tepees were used by the western Plains Indians." She paused, smiling uncertainly.

Allie whispered to Dub, "As any kid who's been through fourth grade could tell you."

To their surprise, Janelle spoke then, saying softly, "Dad, I told you about the longhouses."

Mr. Kavanaugh glanced at her with a frown. "And I believe I told *you*, Janelle, that a tepee is something people will recognize and relate to, whereas who knows anything about longhouses?"

Janelle blushed furiously and stared down at her feet.

Her father turned back to Mrs. Nichols and asked, "So, what have you got for me?"

"I'm afraid I don't have anything like that here at the store," Mrs. Nichols said.

"Anything that looks Indian will work," Mr. Kavanaugh urged.

"Darryl," Mrs. Kavanaugh said quietly, "don't you want to keep it authentic? The local Indians were Senecas, after all. As Ann was saying, their customs were different from those of the Plains Indians."

"We're not building a museum," Mr. Kavanaugh replied impatiently. "We just want an Indian *flavor*. The point is, we want the place to be unique, to have character. To evoke a bygone past."

"It doesn't matter if it's a past that never happened," Dub said softly to Allie, and she smiled and gave him a poke in the side with her elbow.

"I'm afraid I can't help you," Mrs. Nichols said. "I think most relics are actually in museums, or belong to the Senecas themselves. You might have to have someone make reproductions for you to use in your hotel."

Mr. and Mrs. Kavanaugh were turning to leave when Mrs. Nichols said, "You know, this is the first I've heard about a development out at Poplar Point. My understanding was that when the Lucy Stiles Nature Preserve was established at Fossil Glen, it meant that nobody could build there or at the Point."

At the mention of Lucy Stiles and Fossil Glen, Allie gave Dub another nudge. Lucy Stiles had been her first ghost.

"There was a little ambiguity in the wording of that agreement between Mrs. Stiles and the town council," Mr. Kavanaugh said stiffly. "It turns out that, technically, Poplar Point isn't part of the glen. My company's lawyers charged me a small fortune to prove it, too, trust me."

Allie glanced again at Dub, who mouthed the words *Trust you? Fat chance.* She stifled a giggle.

As the Kavanaughs walked past the front desk on their way to the door, Allie experienced a familiar feeling. She prepared herself for what was going to happen next, whether she wanted it to or not. Sure enough, a string of strange words sprang, unbidden, to her lips. They sounded fierce and strong, and very angry.

Mrs. Kavanaugh grasped her husband's arm with a look of alarm. Mr. Kavanaugh cleared his throat and said, "Well. I believe we're finished here. Come along, Janelle."

"Allie," Mrs. Nichols said when they had gone, "what on earth was that all about?"

"Just practicing my lines for the pageant," Allie mumbled.

"You picked a peculiar time to do it," said her mother, before she was called on by another customer seeking help.

"Nice going, Al," said Dub. "You're really good at driving customers away."

"I couldn't help it!" Allie protested. "And they weren't buying anything, anyway. Can you believe Janelle showed up here after stealing my part?"

"Maybe she didn't know this was your mom's store," Dub said. "And if she did, she probably didn't think you'd be here."

"Still, she has a lot of nerve," Allie said with disgust. "She didn't even seem sorry about what she did . . . Although it was weird the way she was hiding behind the coatrack, almost as if she was embarrassed."

"There *is* something weird about the way she acts," Dub said thoughtfully. "She seems nervous all the time. And how come she's always with her parents? Doesn't she have any friends?"

"Who would want to be friends with somebody like her?" Allie asked indignantly.

Dub appeared to be thinking this over, and Allie went on excitedly. "Anyway, Dub, listen. Remember you said that this ghost is real interested in the pageant?" Without waiting for Dub to answer, she said, "The pageant is about Seneca Indians. And every time I blurt out something in that strange language, it's because the subject of Seneca Indians has come up." Her voice grew hushed as she said, "So I'm thinking . . . Well, what are the chances that my ghost is— or was—a real Seneca Indian?"

Dub's eyes had been growing wider with every word from Allie's mouth. "I think," he answered, "now that you say it, the chances are pretty good."

Allie could hear the excitement in his voice.

Then Dub said, "And from the way you just spoke to the Kavanaughs, it's one ticked-off Indian."

Allie laughed. "If we're right, the stuff I'm saying must actually be Seneca!"

"If only we knew what you were saying." Dub was silent for a minute, then asked, "Hey, have you got a portable tape recorder?"

At first Allie was surprised by the change of subject. Then she realized what Dub was getting at. "I think my dad does. He claimed he got these brilliant ideas when he was driving, but that he always forgot them before he had a chance to write them down. He got a recorder so he could tape all his supposed brainstorms, and after that he said he never got another one."

Dub laughed. "Is it small enough so you can carry it around with you?" he asked.

"It fits in a pocket," Allie said.

"So next time you start babbling—"

"I can whip out my trusty recorder and get it on tape!" Allie finished triumphantly. She paused and asked, "*Then* what?"

"Then we find somebody who speaks Seneca to tell us what it means. We take the necessary action, and another ghost bites the dust!" Dub declared triumphantly. Then he shook his head. "Wait, that doesn't make sense. If you're a ghost, you already bit the dust. Anyway, you know what I mean."

"Another ghost rests in peace?" Allie suggested.

"Exactly!"

Allie smiled at Dub and shook her head. "Why do I have the feeling it isn't going to be quite that easy?" she asked.

Eight

Allie and Dub helped at the store until six o'clock. While Mrs. Nichols locked the shop door, they got onto their bikes.

"Mom, is it okay if Dub comes over for dinner?" Allie asked. "There's some stuff we want to do on the computer."

"I don't see why not," her mother answered. "Your father called to say he was cooking hamburgers on the grill. Is that okay with you, Dub?"

"Sure!" said Dub. "I'll call from your house to ask."

"Thanks, Mom," said Allie. "We'll meet you at home."

As they sat out in the back yard eating their burgers, Mrs. Nichols told her husband about her hectic day. "And then something kind of interesting happened," she said. "Darryl and Eileen Kavanaugh came in asking about buying Indian relics to decorate a hotel out at Poplar Point."

Allie couldn't wait any longer to share her news. "Yeah," she said. "And their daughter, Janelle? Today she got my part in the play. I'm just going to be one of the Indian girls, not the narrator."

Her parents looked at her quizzically.

"What do you mean, she got your part?" asked Allie's father.

"Mr. Kavanaugh made Miss Lunsford give her the part. *My* part," Allie said. "And when she got on-stage today, she completely blew her lines *again*."

Allie's father leaned over and gently touched her cheek. "That's terrible, Allie-Cat," he murmured.

"I can't believe Darryl dropped in to the store today after doing that!" said Allie's mother indignantly.

"I don't think he knows I was the one who had the part first," Allie said.

"I don't think he cares, either," declared Dub.

"Wait a second, now," said Mr. Nichols. "What do you mean, Mr. Kavanaugh *made* Miss Lunsford take the part from you?"

Allie shrugged. "He called her boss and the people on the town council and threatened to call the whole thing off unless she gave Janelle the main role."

"I can't imagine the town council allowing themselves to be bullied like that," said Mrs. Nichols.

"Darryl Kavanaugh is throwing a lot of money

around, making all kinds of deals and investments," Mr. Nichols said. "Business in town badly needs a shot in the arm, and the council members know it."

"I'm grateful that Darryl fixed up the building my shop is in," Mrs. Nichols said. "I didn't relish the idea of moving to someplace smaller, or going out of business entirely. But I'm appalled that he would do this. And I was very surprised to hear about his plan to build some sort of hotel center out at Poplar Point. The way he talked about his lawyers, it sounded like a done deal, didn't it?"

Dub nodded in agreement.

At that moment, the image of a girl's face appeared in Allie's mind's eye, fuzzy at first, then becoming clearer and clearer. The girl was young, about Allie's age. Her rich black hair was parted in the center and looked tousled, as if from sleep. Tears fell from her swollen eyes, leaving streaks in the soot and dirt that covered her cheeks. She whispered something Allie couldn't understand, but it sounded like a cry for help.

Allie was entranced by this vision, and was trying to take in every detail, when she heard Michael say, "Allie, who is that girl? Why is she talking funny?"

Allie's breath caught in her throat. She looked at Michael and saw that he was staring into space with a puzzled expression. He could see the girl, too!

Allie's mind raced to come up with an answer that

would satisfy Michael without causing her parents to ask questions, but her brain felt frozen. There was a silence that seemed to Allie to stretch on forever.

Suddenly Dub's glass tipped over and rolled off the table onto the stone patio, where it broke with a loud crash. Milk washed across the table, spilling onto Allie's lap.

"Oh, no!" Dub cried. He jumped out of his chair and knelt down to pick up the pieces, saying, "I'm sorry. I don't know what happened. I just knocked into it . . ."

"Don't touch that glass, Dub," said Mrs. Nichols calmly, rising from her seat and blotting up the milk with some napkins. "You could get cut."

"It was an accident, Dub," Mr. Nichols said. "Don't you worry about it. Allie, grab the dustpan and brush from the kitchen, would you?"

To Allie's relief, by the time they had cleaned up the milk and broken glass, her parents and Michael appeared to have forgotten all about the girl who talked funny. When dinner was over, Allie and Dub escaped to the family room.

Allie looked at Dub with awe. "You are my hero, Oliver James Whitwell!" she exclaimed. "You averted a total disaster with that 'accident' of yours!"

"All it took was fast thinking, lightning-quick re-flexes, and the courage to look like a total klutz," said Dub modestly. "Not to mention the risk of never being invited back for dinner. I hope you appreciate the sacrifices I make for you, Al."

Allie punched his arm and laughed. "I owe you, big-time."

"This is true," Dub acknowledged.

"How did you know what was going on?" Allie marveled.

"All of a sudden you were staring at something with your eyes bugging out, only there wasn't anything there. And then Michael did the same thing," said Dub. "It wasn't hard to figure out. I've been with you when this happened before, remember?"

Allie nodded.

"So was he an Indian?" Dub asked eagerly.

"*She,*" said Allie. "It's a girl. About our age. And, yeah," she went on excitedly, "she could be an Indian, I guess. She had black hair and dark eyes, but it was kind of hard to tell because she was crying. And she was dirty and kind of messy-looking. She said something, which of course I didn't understand."

Dub squinched up his eyes, and Allie could tell he was trying to picture the girl.

"Oh!" said Allie. "That reminds me, I never asked Dad for his tape recorder. I wish I'd had it when she was talking."

"That wouldn't have worked," Dub told her, "because normal people can't hear her, just you and Mike."

"Thanks a lot, Mr. Normal," Allie said dryly.

Dub shrugged. "What can I say?"

"You're right, though," Allie went on. "The tape recorder will only work when she makes *me* say stuff. Stuff that"—she rolled her eyes at Dub—"*normal* people can hear."

"Go get it now," suggested Dub. "Just in case. And I'll see what I can find out about the Seneca language."

After a while Allie returned with the tape recorder to find Dub sitting at the computer table, looking frustrated. She sat beside him, and they continued searching. After an hour they had found a few words written in Seneca, but the spelling was so unusual that they had no idea how the words might sound when spoken.

Finally they found a site with a link that promised audible pronunciation of selected words. They clicked the button eagerly, but got a message saying, "This site is under construction. Please come back later."

"Another dead end," said Dub with disgust, pushing his chair back from the desk. "I can't think of anything else to try."

Allie remembered something then. "Hey, wait a sec," she said. "Miss Lunsford mentioned a restored Seneca village. I can't remember the name exactly, but I think it began with a *G*. She thought maybe there are people there who speak Seneca."

"A *G*?" Dub asked, and began clicking away on the keyboard. After a couple of minutes he said, "Is this it?" He hesitated, speaking the unfamiliar word aloud. "Ganondiyo?"

"Yes!" said Allie.

They were silent as they gazed at the screen, reading. A Seneca village had stood at Ganondiyo until 1687, when it was destroyed by the French. It had been fully restored and featured a visitor center and a full-size replica of a longhouse.

As they browsed the Web site, Mr. Nichols came into the family room and looked over their shoulders.

"I've heard of that place," he said. "It sounds interesting."

"Can we go?" Allie asked impulsively.

Her father read some more. "Hmm," he said. "It's only an hour and a half away. Your mom has to work Saturday, but I could take you. Michael might get a kick out of the longhouse." He smiled and added, "Especially if it's stocked with spears and bows and arrows."

Dub said he'd check with his parents and get back to Allie in the morning at rehearsal.

"Speaking of rehearsal," Dub said as he was leaving, "tomorrow is Friday. We need to record you saying something in Seneca so we can take it to Ganondiyo and get it translated on Saturday."

Allie moaned. "It's hopeless, Dub. Miss Lunsford

expects me not to disrupt rehearsals. If I do blurt something out, the good news is we'll have it on tape. The bad news is I *will* get kicked out."

Dub looked discouraged. Then he brightened. "I have an idea."

"What?" Allie asked warily.

"You could go to Miss Lunsford before rehearsal and tell her you're sorry, and you've changed your attitude about Janelle having your part, and there won't be any more outbursts."

Allie thought it over. "There's no way I've changed my attitude about Janelle. And there probably *will* be more outbursts. In fact, we want an outburst tomorrow so we can record it."

"Yeah," said Dub, sounding discouraged. "I guess it was a dumb idea."

"No, wait. Maybe not," said Allie. "How about this: I go to Miss Lunsford tomorrow and apologize, like you said, for disturbing the rehearsal. And then I tell her we did some research into Seneca words on the Internet, which is true. I just won't mention that we didn't find out anything. Miss Lunsford still wants to use Seneca words, so I'll ask her if it would be okay for me to add some during Janelle's speech." She looked at Dub to see how he would react.

"Okay," he said. "Except how will you know when it's the right time?"

"I *won't*," Allie answered. "I have no control over

these pronouncements, remember? We just have to hope one will pop out so we can record it."

"What if it doesn't?" Dub asked.

Allie shrugged. "If my ghost doesn't make me talk, I'll just babble something."

Dub nodded. "It could work. But Janelle might be a problem. What if she tells her father about you horning in on 'her' part?"

Allie shrugged. "She might. But the way I see it, we've got nothing to lose. And if all goes well, we'll have the words we need on tape."

Nine

Dub left for home, and Allie said good night to her parents and went upstairs. On the way to her room, she stopped to see Michael, who was in bed, surrounded as usual by his Galactic Warrior figures.

"Hi, Mike," she said, curling up beside him. She didn't want to remind him of the girl they had both seen during dinner, since he seemed to have forgotten about her. But things were happening too fast for her to keep up. She was worried that if she went to sleep, she'd have another upsetting dream that Michael would share.

"How about if I sleep in here with you tonight?" she asked.

Michael nodded, his face lighting up. "I'll tell you a story!" he offered.

Michael loved to spin tales about what the good

guys and bad guys in the Galactic Warrior universe were doing. Allie usually listened willingly, amazed at the way he was able to keep track of the personalities and secret powers of so many different characters. She got them all mixed up, no matter how hard she tried to pay attention. Whenever she asked a question to clear things up, Michael would answer patiently, "Because Claw-Girl is a *good* guy, Allie, don't you remember?"

"*I'm* going to tell the story tonight," Allie said.

"Okay," said Michael. He liked hearing stories as much as telling them. "Will it be good guys against bad guys?"

"Absolutely," said Allie, stalling for time. She had the vague idea of telling Michael a story that would help him not be afraid if the ghostly figure appeared again, or if a terrifying dream came to both of them in their sleep. She just had to think of how to do it.

"And a battle?" Michael asked. He loved battles.

"Wait and see," Allie teased. Then she began: "Once upon a time there was a boy named Michael." That was always a safe start.

Michael sighed contentedly and waited to hear more.

"He was one of the good guys," she went on, "and he had superpowers that no one knew about, not even his parents."

Michael smiled at this.

"The only person who knew was his big sister, Allie. It was their secret."

Michael giggled. "What were his secret powers?" he asked.

"Michael saw things nobody else could see. From far, far away, with his super vision, he could see people who were in trouble—"

"Like the crying girl," Michael said matter-of-factly.

"Yes," said Allie. She spoke carefully, trying to make a game of it, knowing that Michael had no way of understanding that the girl he had seen was dead. "Since he was a good guy, Michael wanted to help the girl who was scared and sad."

Michael nodded solemnly.

"So he listened when she talked, even though he didn't understand the language of the planet she came from."

Michael nodded again, and Allie felt herself growing inspired.

"Sometimes Michael saw the people who needed help when he was sleeping. They sent him dreams showing why they were sad and scared. This was when Michael's secret powers came in especially handy." She glanced at Michael, who was listening intently.

"Because then," she went on, "Michael told Allie

all about what he saw, and then she knew how to help the good guys battle the bad guys."

"Michael and Allie are a team," Michael said.

"That's right," Allie agreed. "So you need to be brave if a bad dream comes, okay?"

"Okay," said Michael. His eyes were blinking and trying to close. "Is that the end?" he asked in a sleepy voice.

"Yes," Allie whispered. "Good night." Then she added softly, "Sleep tight."

She could hope, anyway.

Ten

Allie's wish for Michael to sleep peacefully was just that: a wish. Several hours later she woke from a dreadful nightmare, startled and sweating, to find him thrashing and moaning beside her. Quickly she shook him awake and gave him a reassuring hug.

"I had a dream," he mumbled. "Like you said."

"I know," Allie said in what she hoped was a soothing manner. Her own nerves were frayed by the terror she'd felt during her dream, but she didn't want to communicate her unease to Michael. "You want to tell me about it?" she asked after a moment.

Michael's voice was slow and husky from sleep when he answered. "The girl . . . and everybody . . . they were running and crying. There were horses. And the girl . . . she didn't know which way to go. She was looking for her brother and her mother and father near a tree. It was funny-looking."

"What was?"

"The tree," Michael answered patiently. "But she couldn't find them." He paused and thought for a while.

"Anything else?" Allie urged.

"The bad guys were shooting and killing people. Everything was on fire."

Allie nodded. Michael was describing her dream exactly. She'd had the sense that the girl and her family and all the others had been taken by surprise, by a force much more powerful than they. Since they were outnumbered and unprepared to fight back, there hadn't been an actual battle.

She tried to remember the dream in all its detail before it became indistinct, the way dreams do when wakefulness comes and the real world intrudes. Something Michael had said caught in her mind. The girl had been near a "funny-looking tree." Allie, too, had seen this tree in her dream. All of the tree's branches grew upward except for one. Stouter than all the others, it grew downward from the trunk at a peculiar angle. It was familiar, somehow, but she didn't know why.

"Are you okay, Mike?" she asked gently.

Michael nodded. "I was brave," he murmured.

"Yes, you were," Allie said. "Very brave. Now go back to sleep."

Allie lay awake, replaying the dream in her mind,

as Michael's breathing settled into a shallow, steady rhythm.

The girl was the same as the one whose face she'd seen so clearly during dinner. *Was* she a Seneca Indian? Her hair wasn't braided, as Karen's had been in her attempt to look "authentic" for Miss Lunsford. She wasn't wearing a headband, beaded or otherwise. Nor, Allie realized with growing consternation, had her clothing been made of tanned leather hides. She'd been wearing a *dress*; yes, definitely a dress, made of blue calico. No moccasins, either. Her feet had been bare.

Thinking hard, Allie pictured the buildings that were burning. They weren't longhouses but wooden cabins, much like Allie imagined the settlers had lived in.

Unable to sleep, she was overcome with doubt that she and Dub were right about the girl being Seneca. Allie felt as clueless and confused as she had the day the ghost first appeared.

Eleven

On their way to the opera house the following morning, Allie told Dub about the dream she and Michael had shared.

"I sure hope we're not wrong about the ghost being Seneca," he said. "Have you got the tape recorder?"

Allie patted the pouch on the front of her hooded sweatshirt. She'd been glad the morning was cool, because the pocket of the sweatshirt was perfect for hiding the tape recorder. She could easily slip her hand into it to turn the machine on without calling any attention to what she was doing.

"Good. Because it's more important than ever to get some of those words on tape," Dub said. "I mean, if it isn't Seneca you're speaking, we have to start thinking about this thing in a whole different way."

Dub was right. Allie had to record some of her involuntary utterances so that someone could tell her for sure what language it was, and what it meant. That left her in the same impossible position as before. She had to hope that something provoked her ghost to speak through her again, even if she got kicked out of the pageant. With a sigh, she decided she had no choice but to forge ahead with the plan, such as it was, and see what happened.

Nervously she approached the director in the front of the auditorium. "Um, Miss Lunsford, could I talk to you for a second?" she asked.

"Certainly, Allie."

Allie began the apology she had practiced on the way to the theater. "I just wanted to say I'm sorry about my outburst yesterday. It's okay with me that Janelle has my—has the part. I don't mind playing another Indian girl."

Miss Lunsford's eyes grew soft and she smiled. "Thank you, Allie. That was very sweet and very mature of you. To be honest, I didn't blame you for being upset. But I can't have rehearsals being disrupted like that."

"I know," Allie replied. "I was wondering something. Remember you asked me to do some research on the Seneca language? Well, Dub and I did. Would it be okay if I added some Seneca words today during Janelle's speech? Then we can see how they sound."

Miss Lunsford clapped her hands together enthusiastically. "Allie, that is a wonderful idea! Good for you—and Dub." She peered toward the rear of the room and said, "There's Janelle now. We'll tell her." She called, "Janelle! Would you please come here for a moment?"

Janelle approached and stood before Miss Lunsford without a glance at Allie. After Miss Lunsford had explained about the plan for Allie to add some Seneca vocabulary to Janelle's speech, Janelle was silent for a moment. Then, in a low, flat voice, she said, "I think you'd better ask my father."

Allie couldn't believe her ears. Miss Lunsford seemed taken aback as well. She said, "When your mother gave me the script, I told her that artistic changes might be made as we go along. We talked about improvisation. She seemed to understand that theatrical productions usually get tweaked during rehearsals."

"But you'd better check with my father," Janelle said.

Miss Lunsford raised her eyebrows, then said, "Allie, would you excuse us for a moment, please?"

Allie walked over to join Dub, who had been watching the whole exchange anxiously. "What happened?" he asked.

"Unbelievable!" Allie fumed. "I apologized, and

Miss Lunsford was cool with it, but not Janelle." Here Allie paused and adopted a prissy, falsetto tone. "*She* said, 'You'd better ask my father.' "

Dub made a face.

"Like father, like daughter, I guess."

The seats around them had slowly filled with the other kids, and Miss Lunsford called for order. Janelle, eyes downcast, took a seat in front of Allie and Dub.

Miss Lunsford quickly explained to the group that Allie would be inserting some Seneca dialect into Janelle's opening speech. Surprised and relieved, Allie elbowed Dub, murmuring, "Good for Miss Lunsford. I wonder what she said to the Indian princess to keep her from running to her daddy?"

"Shhhh," said Dub, but he elbowed Allie back with a smile.

"Let's do a quick run-through of the scene where the settlers and Senecas first meet," said Miss Lunsford. "Places, please." Dub wasn't in the scene, so he stayed put while Allie, Janelle, and others got up. Allie took her place, reached into her pocket, and pushed the RECORD button. It was a ninety-minute tape, which meant she could record forty-five minutes on one side before turning it over.

Now, instead of fearing another outburst, she was worried that one wouldn't come. But as Janelle stumbled through her lines about the Senecas welcoming

74

the settlers and offering them food, Allie felt the un-mistakable presence of her ghost. And when Janelle finished speaking, Allie gave a speech of her own. She had no idea what it was she'd said, or whether it had been in Seneca or not, but Miss Lunsford was smiling.

Then, later, as they went through another scene in which Janelle spoke of the friendship between the two groups, Allie again spoke out, this time in a fairly long, impassioned speech. Luckily, the timing of both outbursts was perfect, and instead of being angry, Miss Lunsford appeared thrilled with the result.

After rehearsal, when Allie and Dub were alone at last in the alley behind the opera house, she rewound the tape and pushed PLAY. The voices of the other cast members were muffled, but every word that Allie had spoken was just as clear as a bell.

Twelve

Allie curled up beside Michael in his bed again that night. She was afraid to let herself drop into a deep sleep for fear that she—and Michael—would dream. His valiant attempt to be brave the night before had made her heart ache, and she wanted to protect him from the horrible visions as much as she could. So she spent the night drifting off, waking with a start, tossing and turning, and starting the whole cycle again.

Michael bounced up in the morning full of excitement about their visit to the longhouse at Ganondiyo. But Allie could only groan, roll over, and bury her head under the pillow.

Soon her mother was calling up the stairs to say that Dub had arrived. He'd ridden his bike over, just in time to have a second breakfast with Allie and her family. Allie dressed, threw some water on her face, and joined them at the kitchen table. When they'd finished, Mrs. Nichols left for the shop, after complaining good-naturedly about missing all the fun.

"Did you bring the tape?" Dub asked before they got into the car.

Allie nodded. Although she didn't really know what to expect from this visit, she felt excited—now that she was awake. At least they were doing something.

On the drive, Dub and Michael chatted about Iroquois and Seneca weaponry. Michael was thrilled to hear that he might see war clubs in addition to spears and bows and arrows.

At Ganondiyo, they went first to the Visitor Center, where they were greeted by a woman who introduced herself as Ronnie. She was dressed in shorts, sandals, and a T-shirt, and her hair was pulled back in a ponytail.

Michael examined her carefully and said with disappointment, "You're not an Indian."

"Michael!" Allie scolded, embarrassed. She looked apologetically at Ronnie, who just laughed.

"I am of the Seneca nation," she told Michael with a smile. "I belong to the Bear Clan."

Michael's eyes grew big at this.

"You can't always tell us by the way we look," she whispered to him playfully.

Then she told them that since it was a slow morning, she'd take them right out to the longhouse for a tour. As they walked along a trail cut through the sunny meadow, Ronnie explained that the plants that grew by the side of the trail were ones that had significance for the Seneca. They were used for healing, for flavoring food, and for fashioning tools, clothing, and shelter.

While Ronnie talked, Allie became aware of the prickly sensation that signaled the presence of her ghost. She hoped this was a good sign, one that maybe she and Dub were on the right track, after all. Either that, or the ghost was trying to let her know she was wasting her time . . .

They stopped outside the longhouse, where Ronnie explained that, as much as possible, it had been constructed using traditional materials. The frame was made of hickory poles lashed with strips of hickory bark, but some man-made material had replaced the elm bark that was no longer available.

"My people have always been adaptable," she said, smiling again. "That is why we have survived."

Inside, Ronnie gave them a few minutes to explore on their own, saying they could touch anything they wanted, as long as they were respectful. They all stood for a moment, gazing around with interest.

The longhouse was about the size of two school classrooms placed end to end, Allie figured, only the ceiling was higher. Both sides were lined with upper and lower sleeping platforms covered with blankets and furs.

Michael immediately climbed onto one of the lower platforms and burrowed under a buffalo hide. Allie and her father both glanced at Ronnie, who nodded to let them know that was okay.

There were fascinating objects everywhere, and Allie and Dub began examining clay pipes, snowshoes, sleds, canoes, paddles, and lacrosse sticks. Allie showed the sticks to Michael and her dad, since they had a goal set up in their back yard and often played lacrosse together.

Mr. Nichols practiced cradling and made a pretend pass, but Michael had discovered something of even greater interest. On one of the sleeping platforms lay a collection of weapons, including flint knives with bone handles, bows with arrows, spears, war clubs, and muskets. Entranced, Michael picked up and scrutinized each object.

Dub joined him. "Hey, I didn't know Indians had guns," he said.

Overhearing him, Ronnie explained that by the late 1600s, when Ganondiyo had been a thriving village, the Seneca had had years of contact with Europeans, and had adapted many of their tools and materials, including muskets.

She then said she would begin her talk, and that

they could ask questions at any time. She started with a string of words that sounded, at least to Allie, very much like the ones Allie had been spouting during rehearsals. Dub must have thought so, too, because he met her glance with a slight nod.

"I was speaking to you in my language," Ronnie explained. "I introduced myself with my name and my clan, and told you I am a person of the High Hill, or a Seneca. I welcomed you, giving thanks for your good health. I wished you peace and wished for peace between our peoples."

Allie, Dub, and Mr. Nichols each murmured a greeting in return, and Ronnie went on to explain about life in the longhouse. Meanwhile, Allie sensed a strong emotion or agitation coming from her ghost.

When Ronnie finished and asked for questions, Michael announced loudly that he wanted to "play spears."

Mr. Nichols picked Michael up and swung him onto his shoulders, saying, "I think I'll take this young warrior outside for a while and let these two look around some more. Thank you very much, Ronnie. Allie and Dub, take your time."

Alone with Ronnie, Allie glanced at Dub and said, "Well, here goes."

Ronnie looked puzzled, and Allie hesitated. In the heady excitement of having the words on tape in the presence of an actual Seneca person, she hadn't taken the time to consider how she would go about asking to have them translated.

Dub jumped in. "You speak Seneca, right?" Sheepishly, he added, "Duh. I mean, we heard you. The thing is, we have some words we recorded"—at this, Allie removed the tape player from her sweat-shirt pouch—"and we wondered if you could listen to them and tell us if they're in your language. And, if they are, if you could tell us what they mean."

"Who spoke those words on the tape?" Ronnie asked.

Allie looked into Ronnie's kind, open face and asked a question of her own. "Do your people believe in . . . ghosts?"

Dub looked startled, and Ronnie lifted her eye-brows in evident surprise. After a moment, she answered, "We have a saying: 'The dimension that divides the living from the dead is as thin as a maple leaf.'"

Allie contemplated this in silence.

"It is said that some people's spirits continue to wander this earth after death," Ronnie went on. "For some reason, they are unable to follow the path of their journey after life."

"What would make them stay?" Allie asked.

Ronnie was silent. Finally she said, "These are dif-ficult things to talk about."

You're telling me, Allie thought. "I really need to know," she whispered.

Ronnie nodded slowly, then spoke. "Some of these unhappy, earthbound spirits mean no harm. But they can't leave until they are able to settle some matter of earthly business."

Allie and Dub exchanged a glance. What Ronnie was saying about her people's beliefs matched exactly with their own experiences with ghosts.

Ronnie looked troubled, then added in a low voice, "But it is said that some spirits are malicious, and wander the earth in order to do harm."

That, too, Allie and Dub had learned.

"That's why we don't try to summon the spirits of the dead. Who knows what they want or what they will do."

Who, indeed? Allie wondered. Ronnie's words, spoken in hushed tones, brought a sense of foreboding into the shadowy interior of the longhouse.

"Also," Ronnie said, "we have been taught to place our dead into the ground so that their bodies can become part of the sacred earth. If this does not happen, or if a burial site is disturbed, the spirits of the dead are unhappy."

Everyone was quiet for a moment. Then Ronnie said, "But, come. You have a tape. Play it for me."

At that moment, Allie would have done anything Ronnie asked. It was a relief to talk with an adult who appeared to accept that ghosts were real. She pushed the button and for a while they listened to muffled voices and the rustling of Allie's movements. She fast-forwarded a bit to the end of Janelle's opening speech. Then she heard her own voice. When her first speech was over, she stopped the machine.

Ronnie's eyes were bright with interest. "She speaks very well, this girl."

Allie let out a breath she hadn't realized she'd been holding. "So it is your language?" she asked.

"Oh, yes."

"What did she say?" Dub asked eagerly.

"She says her name is Skayendady. Her clan mother would have given her this name. It means 'on the other side of the woodpile.' " Ronnie smiled. "There is a story there, perhaps having to do with her birth."

"Skayendady," Allie repeated slowly.

"She says she is a Seneca of the Wolf Clan," Ronnie continued.

"Wow," said Dub. "So we were right."

"Who is this girl?" Ronnie asked. "Do you know her?"

"Sort of," Allie said evasively. "Wait, there's more."

Other muffled voices spoke, including that of Miss Lunsford giving directions. Then Janelle began her narration again, and afterward Allie's voice came on, strong and clear.

Allie watched as Ronnie's expression grew troubled. When she no longer heard her own voice, Allie stopped the tape. She and Dub waited for Ronnie to speak.

"This is very strange," Ronnie said finally. "Disturbing, really. She says it's a lie, what the speaker before her said. She says she was there, and she knows. There was fire. Many people were killed. Her mother, her father, her little brother, too—she says they all died. Everything was burned." Ronnie stopped, and her dark eyes looked worried.

Allie had the sense that Ronnie was holding something back, and asked quietly, "Is there more?"

"She said *skennon*," Ronnie said, "which means peace or well-being. It is what I wished for you when I first spoke to you in my language. But this girl says there is no well-being. There is no peace."

Allie and Dub stared at each other in wonder. They'd been right. This was truly the ghost of a Seneca girl. And like the other ghosts they had encountered, she could not rest in peace.

After a long silence, Ronnie spoke again. "I have answered your questions. Now it's time for you to answer mine."

Thirteen

"Who is the girl on the tape?" Ronnie asked softly.

Allie and Dub exchanged a glance; his expression told her it was up to her how much she wanted to reveal to Ronnie.

Ronnie hadn't laughed when Allie brought up the subject of ghosts. On the contrary, she had considered Allie's questions seriously. She came from a culture that took for granted the interaction between the spirit world and the earthly world. Allie's questions about ghosts hadn't made Ronnie suggest she see a shrink.

Allie had never told anyone but Dub about her attraction for ghosts, not even her own loving and understanding parents. But telling Ronnie felt different, somehow. Allie looked into Ronnie's eyes and said, "It's my voice on the tape."

Ronnie seemed puzzled. "But—"

"I don't speak Seneca," Allie finished for her. "That's true. This is going to sound very strange, but I promise I'm telling you the truth. What you heard is the voice of a ghost or a spirit, speaking through me."

Ronnie's eyes widened, and she waited for Allie to continue. So Allie explained everything that had happened during the past several months. She watched Ronnie's face for signs of disbelief or scorn, but she saw only interest.

"Anyway, we don't know much about this ghost or what she's like, really, except that we began to think she might be Seneca, which is why we're here," Allie finished.

"There were clues," Dub added. "Like, we're doing this pageant about the history of the Senecas and the settlers in our town, and the ghost showed up the first day of tryouts. And any time someone talked about Indians, this ghost would speak up through Allie. And now we know she's a girl because Allie can see her sometimes, and she sends Allie dreams."

Ronnie nodded. "We believe that dreams come for a reason, to bring messages. Also, I have heard of people who can see spirits." To Dub she said, "Are you one of those people, too?"

Dub grinned. "Nope. I just come along to help— and get scared out of my wits."

"Thank goodness," Allie said.

"Yes," Ronnie said. "This would be a heavy burden to carry alone."

Allie was surprised to feel tears smart at the corners of her eyes. They were tears of gratitude, both for Dub's friendship and for Ronnie's understanding. Allie had been right to trust her.

"But my last dream was confusing," said Allie. "It made me wonder if maybe the girl wasn't Seneca, after all."

"Why?"

Allie described the girl's clothing and the wooden cabins, and Ronnie smiled. "Your brother saw my clothes and thought *I* wasn't Seneca," she said. "People expect us to look like Indians in the movies. This girl's manner of dress and where and how she lived would depend on when she lived. Remember I said that my people adapted to new conditions? They learned to use the tools and materials of the Europeans. They traded for cloth and wool and many other things. So because your dream girl didn't live in a longhouse and wear buckskins doesn't mean she's not Seneca."

Of course, Allie thought, feeling embarrassed by her ignorance.

Allie and Dub were quiet for a moment, as Ronnie appeared to be thinking something over. Finally she said, "Tell me more about this pageant you're doing."

Dub explained that they lived in the town of Seneca, and that this year a pageant had been added to the annual summer festival. "It tells all about the friendship between the first settlers and the Senecas who lived at Poplar Point," he said. "How they shared food and helped each other and stuff like that. The narrator is a girl named Laughs-like-a-waterfall."

Ronnie rolled her eyes. "No Seneca girl would have that name," she said. "It's a name Hollywood would use for an Indian girl in a movie. But it isn't a Seneca name."

Allie smiled, remembering Michael saying the name was "dumb." He'd been right. "To tell you the truth, the whole script is pretty boring," she confided.

"Boring is one thing," Ronnie said quietly. "This script may be something else altogether."

Allie and Dub both looked at her questioningly.

"You heard what Skayendady said. *It is a lie.*"

"A *lie*?" Allie repeated. "I don't understand."

Ronnie sighed. "Well, perhaps the happy friendship you've described between your people and mine did once exist. But if the pageant ends there, it doesn't tell all of what happened at Poplar Point. By leaving out important parts of the story, the pageant doesn't tell the truth."

"What's left out?" Allie asked.

Ronnie's face looked suddenly tired, and sad.

"Have you ever heard of General John Sullivan?" she asked.

Dub and Allie glanced at each other. "The name sounds familiar," Allie said vaguely.

Dub snapped his fingers. "Wait! Isn't he the guy— There's a monument with his name on it. Remember, Al, Mr. Henry showed it to us on our field trip to Fossil Glen?"

"Oh, yeah," said Allie. "It's a big rock with a metal sign on it, and a map."

"He's some kind of hero, right?" Dub asked Ronnie.

Ronnie smiled gently. "I suppose that depends on your point of view."

"What did he do?" asked Allie. "I can't remember."

"Come," said Ronnie, settling herself so that she sat cross-legged on one of the lower sleeping platforms. She patted a deerskin on her left and a woolen blanket on her right. "Sit. I will tell you the story. I believe Skayendady wishes you to know it."

Eagerly Dub and Allie crawled onto the platform with Ronnie and made themselves comfortable. Outside, the sun must have disappeared behind a cloud, as the dim, shadowy interior of the longhouse grew even darker.

"Imagine, if you can, the fright and confusion of

my people when the pale-skinned ones from Europe first came—and kept coming."

Allie and Dub nodded.

"Perhaps you can imagine how strange the ways of these Europeans were to us. They not only warred against us at times, but were continually fighting among themselves as well. My people were caught up in these wars between the white people and forced to take sides, even though they couldn't possibly understand what was at stake.

"When your Revolutionary War came along, the Senecas and most of the other tribes in the Iroquois Confederacy sided with the British, not the colonists. Did you know that?"

Dub shook his head, and so did Allie. If she had learned it, she'd forgotten.

"In 1779, the commander of the colonists, George Washington, ordered his general, John Sullivan, to punish the tribes who were friends with the British."

Allie knew that the next part of the story was not going to be good, and she began to get a churning feeling in the pit of her stomach. She was suddenly aware, too, of the spirit of Skayendady hovering nearby, drawn perhaps by the telling of a tale she undoubtedly knew too well.

"How did he punish them?" Allie asked quietly.

"Sullivan's orders were to eliminate any possible threat that might come from the Iroquois—or 'the hostiles,' as he called them. So he and his troops marched westward across New York State, doing everything they could to wipe out the Iroquois forever."

Allie remembered now. The map on the plaque showed Sullivan's route on this journey.

"They killed the people whenever they could, and laid waste to their villages, homes, crops, and orchards so that they could never rise up and prosper again," Ronnie continued in a sad, soft voice.

Allie shivered, although the longhouse held the warmth of summer. "But why did they build him a monument for doing that?"

Ronnie shrugged. "It's part of your history. It was meant to be the end of *our* history"—she gave the ghost of a smile—"but, as you see, some of us survived."

But not Skayendady, Allie thought. Vivid images from her dreadful nightmares came back to her, and she was sure that she knew the meaning of the dreams. "Sullivan's men went to Poplar Point, didn't they?" she asked.

Dub looked startled, then turned to Ronnie for her answer.

Ronnie nodded. "They spotted the village at Poplar Point from the other side of the lake, and they went to destroy it. They burned the homes. They set fire to the fields of corn and beans, squash and melons, and to the orchards filled with peaches and apples. Horses, chickens, pigs, men, women, and children—all were wiped out. They never knew it was coming."

Allie had seen this happening in her nightmare. Now, once again, she could see Skayendady's tear-and-dirt-streaked face, and the terror in her eyes. She could hear the screams of the people and of the horses. She could feel their panic at finding themselves under murderous attack.

No wonder Skayendady's spirit can't rest in peace, she thought.

From outside the longhouse they heard Michael shriek with laughter. The sun came back out, and beams of light streamed once again through the openings at the roof. Allie, Dub, and Ronnie, still under the spell of the past, were jolted back to the present. They looked at one another for a moment without speaking.

Then Dub sat up straighter and said, "Al, remember when we were at your mom's shop and Mr. Kavanaugh was talking about building his 'Indian-theme' hotel at Poplar Point?"

"Yes," said Allie. She thought, but didn't say, that the discussion had made Skayendady very angry.

"Tell me more about this," Ronnie said with interest.

Allie and Dub told her about Mr. Kavanaugh's

plan and about his request for Indian artifacts to decorate the lobby and restaurant.

Ronnie said, "He wants to build a hotel at Poplar Point, where my ancestors were slaughtered?"

Allie felt a shock of horror at the question. She and Dub both nodded unhappily.

"He wants to build this hotel with an 'Indian theme' on the site of an Indian *massacre*?" Ronnie asked incredulously.

The terrible word hung in the silence of the longhouse.

Fourteen

Allie and Dub's time with Ronnie was cut short when other visitors arrived. Michael was hungry and ready to go, anyway. As they were leaving, Ronnie quickly slipped Allie a business card, saying, "If I can help you further, just call."

Allie pocketed the card gratefully. "Thank you so much."

Back at the Nicholses' house, Dub and Allie sat in the family room talking. "I sure didn't expect you to tell Ronnie . . . you know, about seeing ghosts and all," said Dub. "But I'm glad you did."

"Me too," said Allie. "She was so nice. And such a big help. I mean, we understand much more now than we did before." After a pause she added, "What I *can't* understand is if Skayendady died in 1779 in the raid at Poplar Point, why did she wait until now to appear?"

Dub looked thoughtful. "This all began with the pageant," he ventured. "Maybe Skayendady is, well, kind of riled up now because the story is being told wrong."

Allie nodded. It made sense that Skayendady's spirit could have drifted in misery for over two hundred years, then been driven to act by the pageant.

Dub went on. "Ronnie said that the Senecas believe in returning their dead to the earth. But I doubt Sullivan's men bothered to bury the people they killed at Poplar Point."

"I wonder what happened to their bodies," Allie said.

"They probably just rotted where they lay," Dub answered. "Animals would come and spread the bones around. Slowly, any bones left behind would sink into the soil, and be covered by leaves and stuff." Dub made a face and added, "Not exactly a proper burial."

They were both silent for a moment. "Skayendady showed up when the pageant rehearsals began—a pageant that was Mr. Kavanaugh's idea, and that Skayendady says is a lie," Allie said finally. "Right at the same time, Mr. Kavanaugh was getting permission to build his hotel at Poplar Point."

"It all points to him," Dub said. "He's the reason Skayendady showed up now."

"He must not know what happened at Poplar

Point," Allie mused aloud. But then, thinking about Mr. Kavanaugh, she wasn't sure about that. "If he doesn't know, somebody needs to tell him."

Dub looked at her and smiled. "Good idea. Go for it."

"Oh, sure," Allie said with a laugh. "Since he's shown himself to be such a pleasant, reasonable person."

"Or—I know! How about if we talk to Janelle?" Dub suggested. "We'll tell her what we found out—"

Allie broke in sarcastically, "And our dear friend Janelle will do all she can to help. Where's the phone book? Let's call her right now."

They sat for a minute, quiet and discouraged. Then Dub said, "Okay, we know there's, like, zero chance Mr. Kavanaugh's going to listen to *us* about this. He probably wouldn't even talk to us. But we might have a shot at Janelle. And if we convince her, maybe she'll be able to talk to her father."

Allie looked at him skeptically.

He met her gaze. "You got a better idea?"

Allie had to admit that she didn't. She stood up and came back with a phone book, reached into her pocket, and pulled out a quarter. "Heads, you call. Tails, I do."

Dub nodded. Allie tossed the quarter into the air and let it fall. She moaned. It was tails. Dub made an effort to appear sympathetic, but Allie could see the relief on his face.

"This *is* crazy," she said. "Janelle's just like her father."

"Tell her the story, the way we heard it from Ronnie," Dub urged. "Come on. She'd have to have a heart of stone not to feel *something*."

"I wish she could have heard it from Ronnie instead of me," Allie said. Then she looked up the Kavanaughs' number, took a deep breath, and dialed.

To her relief, Janelle answered the phone. She sounded surprised when Allie identified herself. Not wanting to give Janelle any chance to hang up, Allie hurriedly told her about the trip to Ganondiyo. She poured out the whole story in a rush, without a break, and when she had finished, there was silence on the other end of the phone.

"Janelle?" she said uncertainly. "Are you there?"

"Yes," Janelle answered. She sounded equally uncertain.

"Well," Allie said, "can you help us? Tell your parents what I just told you. Maybe you can convince your father to change the pageant. It's really important."

"No," Janelle whispered.

"No?" Allie repeated.

"I can't," Janelle said. Her voice was low and expressionless.

"You mean you won't!" Allie said in a flash of anger.

Janelle said quickly, "Look, I've got to go—"

Allie heard a click and then the dial tone. She hung up her receiver. "Well, now we know: she does have a heart of stone."

"What did she say?" Dub asked.

"She said *no*," Allie replied. "And *I can't*. Other than that, she was very understanding and helpful."

Dub shrugged. "It didn't hurt to try."

"I just don't get her," Allie said with frustration. "She doesn't care about what happened to Skayendady and her family. She doesn't care if the pageant is nothing but a bunch of lies, as long as she gets the starring part her father bullied people into giving her! She doesn't even seem to care that she has no friends, as long as she doesn't upset Daddy." She fell onto the couch beside Dub, drained.

"Feel better now?" Dub asked half-jokingly.

"No. We've accomplished exactly nothing to help Skayendady, and I'm fresh out of ideas." She shook her head tiredly. "I'm dying for a good night's sleep."

Being a ghost magnet was exhausting.

Fifteen

Allie spent the night in Michael's room again, not allowing herself to sleep deeply so she—and therefore Michael—wouldn't have nightmares. When he awoke in the morning and went downstairs, Allie burrowed under the covers, thinking she'd get some actual rest at last. But after less than five minutes, Michael was back.

"Allie!" he called loudly. "Wake up! Telephone!"

She sighed, emerged from under Michael's brightly colored Galactic Warriors bedspread, and went down the hallway to her parents' bedroom. She picked up the phone and croaked, "Dub Whitwell, you better have a really good reason to be calling me this early."

But it wasn't Dub.

It was Janelle. "Listen," she whispered urgently.

"I've only got a second. My mother's in the shower and my father went out to the curb to get the paper. He can't know I'm calling you."

"Why?" Allie said, struggling to fully wake up.

Janelle went on, speaking so fast Allie had to concentrate to hear every word. "When you called yesterday, my father was listening on the other phone. You were talking, so you didn't hear him pick up, but I did. That's why I couldn't say anything."

Allie was having trouble taking in what Janelle was saying, partly because she was still blurry from sleep, and partly because she couldn't imagine her own father listening in on her phone calls. "Why did he do that?" she asked.

Janelle let out an exasperated sigh. "Because it's just the way he *is*. He's, like, in control of everything."

Including you, thought Allie, feeling fully awake now. She was quiet, though, wanting to hear what Janelle had to say next.

"What you said, it was news to me. But my father already knew all about it," Janelle went on hurriedly. "And he says it's ancient history. He says everybody's forgotten about it, and nobody on the town council said one word about it when he first made his proposal to build out there. He says bringing it up and reminding people would be bad for business, and people in town are counting on the jobs and money the hotel is going to bring in." She paused for a moment to catch her breath and added, "He was *so* mad."

Allie waited to hear more.

"And then my mom said that if there was a massacre at the Point, it means the pageant is a fraud. And my dad told her she was overreacting, and the pageant is just fine the way it is. He says there's nothing wrong with showing how the settlers and Indians met, and what happened later is another story—one nobody needs to hear.

"And Mom got really upset, and they had a huge fight. I went into my room after a while so I didn't have to listen. But I heard my father say that no little brats are going to ruin his plans, and the pageant is going to go on the way it is, and so are the plans for the hotel."

Allie felt a chill. The "little brats" were her and Dub. "But how can he—" she began.

"Look," Janelle interrupted. In a pleading voice, she said, "You don't know my father. When he decides something, it happens." She was still talking very quickly, obviously afraid of being caught. "I know you hate me for getting your part, but you've got to listen. I thought about this all night. There's no use going against my father. The best thing to do is follow along with the pageant the way it is, and keep your mouth shut. I mean, who will it hurt? Is there really anybody who cares about what happened in this town more than two hundred years ago?"

Janelle broke off, and Allie heard a voice calling in the background, "Janelle?"

Janelle gasped. "Gotta go."

And the line went dead.

Allie stood for a moment, stunned, the phone in her hand. Forgetting all about sleep now, and about how she hadn't wanted to be called so early on a Sunday morning, she dialed Dub's number.

Luckily, Dub was an early riser, and he answered the phone. When Allie told him about the phone call from Janelle, he was as upset as she. "What do we do now?" he asked.

"I don't know," Allie answered. "But her father called us brats!" Then, after her indignation had passed, she added, "He already knew all about the massacre! He's just mad that we know because we might mess up his precious project."

"Unbelievable," said Dub.

"The whole conversation was so weird," Allie said slowly.

"I bet. You must have been really surprised when she called."

"It wasn't just that," Allie replied. "I'm still not

sure *why* she called. I mean, at first I thought it was because she's just like her father and was trying to help him by telling us to back off. But now I'm beginning to think . . ." She struggled to explain. "It was like she was scared. Of her own father! She was absolutely terrified of getting caught talking to me. And it was like she called to warn us because she's afraid of what he might do, and thinks we should be, too."

Dub seemed to think this over. Then he said, "I see what you mean. But what can he do to us?"

"Good question," said Allie. "I have no idea." She sighed. "So what do we do now?"

"Let's go out to Poplar Point," Dub said impulsively.

"For what?" asked Allie.

"I don't know. We'll see what's going on, how far the project has gone. Maybe we'll think of something when we get there. And, besides, we haven't been in the lake yet this summer."

Allie doubted they'd accomplish anything by going to the Point, but it was a beautiful day and she loved swimming there.

"Okay," she said. "Come over in an hour and bring your suit." She hung up the phone and went down the hallway to her room. As she got dressed, she thought about Janelle's question: *Is there really anybody who cares about what happened in this town more than two hundred years ago?*

"Yes!" Allie said out loud. She was thinking about Skayendady, but as soon as she said it, she realized she meant herself as well.

Sixteen

While Mrs. Nichols was making her special Sunday-morning-in-summer blueberry pancakes, Allie asked if she could bike out to Poplar Point with Dub for a swim.

Her father replied, "Better go while you can."

"What do you mean?" Allie asked.

"If Darryl Kavanaugh's company builds out there, I imagine only hotel guests will be welcome," Mr. Nichols said.

"That stinks!" Allie said indignantly. "I've been swimming there my whole life."

"Some of us would have brought that up at the town council meeting, if we'd known there was a meeting," her dad said wryly.

Mrs. Nichols brought Allie a plate of pancakes. Frowning, she said, "It's very odd the way that hotel project was rushed through the town council. I didn't even hear about it until three days ago, when it had already been approved." She spooned more batter into the frying pan and murmured, "It's all happening so fast."

"At the longhouse, Dub and I learned that an entire village of Seneca Indians was massacred at Poplar Point. Do the council members know about that?" Allie wondered aloud.

"If they know, I imagine they don't like to think about it, Allie-Cat," her father answered. "To most people, what's happening today is more important."

"I wonder what it would take to wake the town up to its own history?" Mrs. Nichols mused. "Everyone appears to be more concerned about the money the resort will bring to the area."

"And into Darryl Kavanaugh's pocket," Mr. Nichols said, adding, "He's certainly not doing all this for the 'good of the town.'"

"I don't like him," Allie declared. "He's creepy."

"Allie!" admonished her mother.

"Well, he is. He bosses everybody around. The town council, Miss Lunsford, everybody acts scared of him, even his own daughter." Allie didn't mention her phone call from Janelle. She wanted to go to Poplar Point with Dub and didn't want to give her parents any reason to worry.

Mrs. Nichols looked thoughtful and Mr. Nichols

said, "You know, Allie, I'm glad you brought all this up. I think I'll ask around and see what I can find out. Maybe it's not too late for the council to reconsider."

"Good," said Allie.

"Michael!" Mrs. Nichols called. "Your pancakes are done!"

"So, is it okay if I go to Poplar Point with Dub?" Allie asked.

"I don't see why not," said her father.

"I wish we could all go," said Mrs. Nichols. "But your father and I are going to try to actually finish the patio today." For weeks, Allie's parents had been spending Sundays working on the project.

"I'm helping," announced Michael, coming into the room. "I'm mixing cement."

"You sure are, big guy," said Mr. Nichols. "So you need to eat a good breakfast."

"You and Dub be careful," Mrs. Nichols said as she handed Michael a plate of pancakes. "Don't go out too deep."

"Mom," said Allie. "You know how shallow it is there. You have to walk out forever before it's even up to your waist." She excused herself before her mother could think of any more warnings, and got ready to leave with Dub.

The road to Poplar Point passed right by the monument the state had erected to General John Sullivan, and Allie and Dub stopped to examine it. The dull, dry words on the plaque conveyed no emotion or drama. No mention was made of the massacre that had taken place just a quarter mile away. Allie reflected that it was no wonder everyone seemed to have forgotten all about it.

Back on their bikes, Allie and Dub crossed the bridge over the creek that flowed through Fossil Glen, and followed the dirt road that ran alongside the creek and out to Poplar Point. Willow and poplar trees hung over the bank of the creek, and Allie watched minnows darting about in the shade. It was a beautiful place, and one of the few parcels of land on the lakefront that remained undeveloped. Allie hated to think of a big hotel complex there, keeping her and others out.

Then she saw it: the "funny-looking" tree with the downward-pointing branch she and Michael had seen in their dreams. That's why it had seemed familiar; she had seen it many times at Poplar Point. It was a huge, majestic oak that had to be well over two hundred years old.

But today there was something different about it. A blaze orange strip of plastic was tied around the trunk.

"Look!" Dub said, pointing to a large sign. "That's new."

Allie read the sign:

COMING SOON!
LAUGHING WATERS RESORT AND
CONFERENCE CENTER
THREE SISTERS RESTAURANT
GREAT TREE MARINA
LAKE COUNTRY DEVELOPMENT GROUP
DARRYL KAVANAUGH, V.P.,
NEW YORK PROPERTIES

"Laughing Waters Resort, Three Sisters Restaurant," Allie said scornfully. "How hokey is that?"

"Yeah, as if they're going to serve corn, beans, and squash," Dub agreed.

"Look at those." Allie indicated some wooden stakes, also tied with blaze orange strips, which were stuck into the ground at various places all over the Point.

"Survey markers," Dub said. "And a bulldozer and an excavating machine. It looks like they've done a little digging, too."

Allie stared at the tree, which stood in the midst of the survey markers. If the stakes marked the boundaries of the hotel, the ancient tree that had witnessed the killing of Skayendady and her family and the destruction of her village was tagged for removal. Allie felt sick, and deeply angry.

"I wonder if they've dug up any bones?" Dub said in a hushed voice.

"Maybe even Skayendady's bones," Allie murmured. The thought made her shiver. After a moment she said gloomily, "Dad says we'd better swim while we can. The way it looks, he's right."

"First," said Dub, "we have work to do."

Allie watched, puzzled, as he removed his backpack. He rummaged inside, took out markers and some pieces of stiff cardboard, and held them up. "I had an idea," he said. "We'll make signs and put them up here to let people know what's going on."

"Dub," Allie said with a giggle, "are you serious?"

"Sure," he replied. "Why not? It might draw a little attention to what's happening. And it's not vandalism or anything. Just a few pieces of paper, that's all."

"Diabolical, Mr. Whitwell!" Allie declared. She took a marker and a piece of cardboard, knelt on the ground, and thought for a minute. Then she wrote in large block letters:

SITE OF A SENECA MASSACRE

Dub knelt beside her. He wrote:

HERE OUR ANCESTORS WERE MURDERED IN 1779
The Seneca People

"Excellent!" said Allie. "I know! How about—"
She broke off abruptly as a shadow appeared over her

shoulder. Still kneeling, she turned and gazed up into the glaring sun, against which she could make out the figure of a man. She stood quickly, the cardboard falling from her hands. Dub rose as well, and they stood looking into the stony face of Darryl Kavanaugh.

"Allie, isn't it?" he said. "And Dud?"

"*Dub,*" said Dub, sounding annoyed.

"Just what do you kids think you're doing?" he asked in a flat voice that frightened Allie more than if he'd shouted.

She glanced quickly at Dub, who looked every bit as rattled as she felt. Neither of them spoke.

Mr. Kavanaugh went on. "Never mind. I can see for myself."

Watching him, Allie thought that he might be handsome, except for the coldness in his eyes.

Mr. Kavanaugh let out a loud sigh. Then he loosened his tie and put his hands casually into the pockets of his neatly pressed trousers.

He appeared, Allie thought uneasily, as if he were planning to settle in for a chat.

"It sure is hot," he said after a while. "Nice day for a swim."

It wasn't a remark that called for an answer, and Allie didn't say anything. Dub, still scowling, didn't either.

Mr. Kavanaugh spoke again. "You know, when I

first came to Seneca, there were a lot of empty store-fronts and a lot of buildings that were pretty run-down. I've fixed them up, as I believe you—and your parents—know."

Allie didn't say anything. There was no point in denying the truth.

"You see," he went on, "I have a vision for this town."

He smiled, but Allie didn't sense any warmth or friendliness in it.

"Now, I know you two have got yourselves all riled up about things that happened out here over a couple hundred years ago. Maybe you think your little signs will get other people riled up, too. But I'm willing to bet folks care a lot more about having jobs and nice stores to shop in, and about bringing new business to town, than they do about ancient history. This hotel I'm building—and, believe me, I *am* going to build it—will bring a lot of new business and a lot of money to this area. That's what people want. That's what they care about. I've invested a lot of money already to make sure they *get* what they want."

He looked down at the ground for a minute, then up at Allie and Dub with a penetrating gaze.

"Do you understand what I'm telling you? In all my negotiations and discussions about this project, no one, not one person, has brought up this"—he grimaced with distaste—"massacre business. Nobody cares. And I don't think they'll take kindly to anybody who tries to drum up trouble about it."

Mr. Kavanaugh reached out then and put one hand on Allie's shoulder and the other on Dub's. "So, a word to the wise, eh? Enjoy the summer, have a good time at the festival, put on a great pageant, and forget all this foolishness."

He picked up the cardboard signs and ripped them in half, giving Allie and Dub another smile that wasn't really a smile.

This time Allie read triumph in his eyes. She glanced quickly at Dub, who was staring open-mouthed at Darryl Kavanaugh. Neither she nor Dub said a word until Mr. Kavanaugh strode stiffly away.

"Dub," Allie said in a near whisper, "does he scare you?"

Dub nodded slowly.

"Me too." After a moment she said, "And I hate the way he talks to us, like we're dumb little kids."

Dub nodded again. "Makes me mad."

Allie agreed. But being mad felt better than being meek and frightened. "Come on," she said with determination. "We came here to swim, so let's swim."

Ordinarily they would have raced each other into the water, but the encounter with Mr. Kavanaugh had left them subdued. They stripped down to their bathing suits and walked into the shallow water near shore. A mama mallard swam away squawking noisily, her brood of ducklings scooting along behind her.

Then they had the Point to themselves. It was quiet except for the splashing of their feet, the sound of the waves lapping gently on the shore, and the rustle of the breeze through the grass and low brush at the shoreline. Occasionally a laugh or shout carried across the sparkling water from swimmers, water-skiers, and sunbathers enjoying a peaceful Sunday afternoon.

They waded out to deeper water and swam until they were covered in goose bumps, then ran to shore, gasping. Spreading out their towels, they lay down and let the warmth of the sunbaked gravel seep into their chilled bodies.

On her back with her eyes closed, Allie felt Skayendady's spirit hovering nearby, and she let her mind drift to meet it. Although they were separated by death and by the passing of two centuries' time, Allie and Skayendady were both young girls. Both had friends and a mother and a father and a younger brother they loved.

Allie tried to imagine Skayendady's pain at seeing her family killed. It was too awful to contemplate. She had asked herself why Skayendady had come to her for help. Lying at the place where Skayendady had spent her final moments, Allie thought she had the answer. It was to make sure the people of Seneca remembered what had happened back in the earliest beginnings of their town on the shores of the lake. It was to make sure they realized who had come before them, and that they felt at least a little of Skayendady's timeless sorrow. And it was to make sure Skayendady and those who died with her could rest in peace.

Allie let the images from her nightmares fill her mind. Then she thought of the pretty picture painted by Mr. Kavanaugh's pageant. She heard the lifeless narration and dull dialogue, saw the happy scenes of generosity and friendship. A boring—and shame-less—lie.

She remembered the question her mother had asked that very morning: *I wonder what it would take to wake the town up to its own history?*

Allie sat up.

"Hey! You're blocking my sun," protested Dub. He peered at her from half-closed eyes.

"Dub!" she said slowly. "I have an idea."

"Oh, no." Dub groaned. "This means trouble. Look, I gotta go. I hear my mother calling me."

Allie swatted his arm. "I'm serious!"

"So am I," said Dub, sitting up now, too. "This is where I should put my hands over my ears and hum very loudly until you stop talking. But do I learn? No."

Allie giggled, but an idea was taking shape in her

mind, and she could barely contain her excitement. "You're going to like this, honest," she said. "Mr. Kavanaugh says people in town don't know and don't care about the massacre. Well, how about if we make sure they do know?"

"How?" Dub asked.

"Say we add a new ending to the pageant? One that tells the truth."

Dub looked skeptical. "I gotta ask again, Al. How?"

"You know how you're the last one onstage, giving Cornplanter's big speech?"

Dub nodded cautiously.

"Well, suppose you say something completely different from the script? Something about what *really* happened. And then you and I and some of the other kids—Joey, Brad, Pam, and Julie, say—take over the stage and we act out the massacre in front of the whole town! I'll play Skayendady and show how she was killed."

Allie stopped, flushed with excitement, and waited for Dub's reaction.

He shook his head and said flatly, "I've got to say, Al, I think this ghost business is finally getting to you. That is the craziest, most outrageous, most ridiculous, most whacked-out idea you've ever come up with."

Allie was crestfallen. "You don't like it?"

"Are you kidding?" Dub shouted. "I love it!"

"Really?" Allie shrieked.

"I can just picture the look on Mr. Kavanaugh's face!" Dub said with a grin.

Allie stared at him wide-eyed. "Do you think we can pull it off?"

"Miss Lunsford did say she's all for improvisation," Dub said, adding, "although this probably isn't quite what she had in mind."

"We could get into a whole lot of trouble," Allie said soberly. "And Mr. Kavanaugh is going to freak."

"Yeah," Dub agreed. "But I can tell you one thing . . ."

Allie looked at him cautiously.

"It will *not* be boring!"

Seventeen

The next morning, rehearsal at the opera house went on as usual, except for two things. First, Allie and Dub told Miss Lunsford that they had visited Ganondiyo and learned that Laughs-like-a-waterfall was a phony name for a Seneca girl. When they suggested Skayendady as a replacement, Miss Lunsford said it was an excellent idea and announced the change to the rest of the cast.

Then, shortly afterward, Darryl Kavanaugh entered the theater and sat down in the last row. He watched in silence until Allie began speaking her first lines of Seneca dialogue. Then he leaped to his feet and interrupted, saying, "Hold it. What was *that*?"

When Miss Lunsford explained that they had added bits of the Seneca language for authenticity, he shook his head. "No," he said flatly. "No Indian gibberish. The audience won't have any idea what it means."

"But—" Miss Lunsford began.

"I said no," Mr. Kavanaugh said.

Miss Lunsford appeared too stunned to speak. After a moment, Mr. Kavanaugh said, "Go ahead. Continue. In English."

Miss Lunsford took a deep breath before saying quietly, "You heard Mr. Kavanaugh, people. Let's go on, without the Seneca dialogue, please, Allie."

Allie looked at Dub and rolled her eyes. *Oh, well,* she thought, *so much for trying to be authentic.* She glanced at Janelle to see how she was reacting, but Janelle was staring steadfastly at the floor. Allie felt acutely aware of her, as if an invisible thread ran between them. She was sure Janelle felt it also, but was too intimidated by her father to even look in Allie's direction.

It was a shame to lose the Seneca words, but Allie was too excited about what was going to happen after rehearsal to dwell on it.

As soon as Miss Lunsford dismissed them, Allie, Dub, Pam, Julie, Brad, and Joey walked together to Dub's house. Allie outlined the plan as they all sat under the big oak tree in the Whitwells' yard with their lunch bags.

Dub brought out a carton of lemonade and some paper cups. Brad took a big gulp of lemonade and stifled a belch. "That reminds me," he said. "I called Uncle Hal last night after you called me, and he said he has the stuff you want, no problem."

"Cool!" said Dub.

"I told you he'd come through," Brad said proudly.

"Wait, what stuff are you talking about?" asked Pam.

"Yeah, hold on. I'd like to know exactly what's going on," said Julie. "Can you guys tell us the whole plan, from the start?"

Allie looked at Dub, who nodded for her to begin. "Well, we haven't really figured out the whole plan," she said. "Right now it's a little sketchy." *Boy, is that the truth,* she thought. "We're hoping, actually, that you guys will come up with some ideas—"

Allie was interrupted by Joey shouting, "Hey! What are you doing, sneaking around here?"

They all looked up to see Karen Laver smirking at them over the hedge that bordered the front of the Whitwells' yard. "It's a public sidewalk, Joey. I'd hardly call it sneaking. And anyway, your voice is so loud the whole neighborhood can hear you."

Allie was awed by Karen's ability to respond in the form of an attack, even when caught in the act of spying on them.

"Awww, gee, guys," said Dub, looking crestfallen. "We're busted. Now Karen knows . . ."

Karen's face lit with triumph, and Dub went on,

". . . all about our secret afternoon meetings of the Karen Laver Fan Club."

Everybody laughed except Karen, who scowled.

"Maybe you could give us a suggestion, Karen," Dub went on. "See, we're having trouble finding a room small enough for the meetings."

"Ha ha ha," Karen said. "So, what's the stupid little plan you were talking about?"

"There's no plan," said Allie.

"Give it up, Allie. I heard enough to know there is one. And I'm going to find out what it is."

"Knock yourself out," said Dub. "And I mean that sincerely."

Karen wiggled her fingers and turned to walk away. "Bye-bye, now. Don't forget, I'll be watching."

"Whew," said Brad when she was out of sight. "That was close."

"She is definitely looking for trouble," said Dub.

Pam glanced around nervously, as if Karen might still be skulking about. "Is it okay to talk now?" she asked.

Brad said, "She's gone."

"So, basically, you're talking about adding a scene to the pageant, right?" asked Pam. "A surprise ending?"

Allie tried to put Karen out of her mind and get on with the plan. "Exactly. See, the way it is, the pageant doesn't tell the whole story. It makes it seem like the settlers and the Indians lived happily ever after."

"But that guy Sullivan and his soldiers slaughtered them," Joey broke in, in his usual booming voice. "And that's where we come in!" He held up a pretend musket and "fired" it. "Blam! Blam! Blam!"

"Shhh!" said Julie. "Karen was right about one thing, Joey. You've got to keep it down."

"Joey," Allie added, "this isn't like a video game or something. It was real. We want to show how horrible it was."

"Well, sure," said Joey, looking slightly abashed. "I know."

Brad, grinning, asked, "But we can still have a blast doing it, right? Get it? A *blast*?"

Allie looked to Dub for help.

"Definitely," Dub said. "Especially if Uncle Hal gets us the starting pistols and smoke bombs! But listen, guys, Allie's right: the whole point is to show what really happened. And it wasn't pretty."

"Okay, okay," said Brad. "We got it."

"Can I be Sullivan?" Joey asked. "I can be a really good bad guy."

"Sure," said Allie. She smiled to herself. One thing was certain, Joey's voice would have no trouble carrying to the entire audience. "But there's one other important thing you should know . . ."

Joey, Brad, Julie, and Pam looked at her warily.

"Mr. Kavanaugh—you know, Janelle's father, the

guy whose company is paying for the pageant—is not going to be happy about this. Which is why we can't take a chance on Karen finding out. And why we can't tell anybody what we're doing ahead of time."

"Not even Miss Lunsford?" asked Julie.

"Nobody."

"Nobody except Uncle Hal," Brad said. "I had to tell him. And we can totally trust him."

"I don't get how we're going to pull it off if nobody knows about it but us," Pam said.

Allie looked at Dub. It *was* a problem. "We haven't figured out all the details yet," she said. "But we have to get started. Some things we'll just have to work out as we go along."

Dub nodded encouragingly. The truth was, if they worried about all the holes in the plan, they'd never get anywhere.

"And," Allie went on, "I just want to warn you. We might get into trouble with Mr. Kavanaugh."

There was silence for a minute. Then Julie said, "What kind of trouble?"

"I don't know exactly," said Allie. "But he said some scary things to me and Dub. He owns practically everything in town. He could—I don't know . . ." Her voice faltered.

"What?" Joey asked scornfully. "What can he do to us?"

"Oooh, I'm scared," said Brad in a high, fluttery voice.

"Why would we get into trouble for telling the truth?" asked Pam.

"Mr. Kavanaugh doesn't seem to care very much about the truth," Allie explained. "All he cares about is making money."

"And he figures everybody else feels the same way," added Dub.

"Well, he's wrong!" declared Pam.

"What's with his daughter, anyway?" asked Julie. "She isn't very friendly."

"She's probably just like her father," Brad answered with a shrug.

"Then we'd better make super sure *she* doesn't find out what we're doing," Julie said.

Although Allie was no longer certain Janelle was "just like her father," she agreed with Julie that Janelle must not get wind of their secret plan. Janelle's fear of her father made her unpredictable, and that was dangerous. *As if we didn't have enough to worry about with Karen,* Allie thought.

"Julie's right," she said aloud. "We need to be really careful. Now let's get to work!"

Eighteen

During the rest of the week, Allie had no bad dreams, experienced no sudden visions, and made no embarrassing pronouncements in the Seneca language. Finally she felt it was safe to return to her own bed. She was relieved for Michael's sake, and also for her own, as she was finally getting some sleep.

It was as if, she thought, Skayendady had backed off, understanding that Allie was doing everything she could to help.

The pageant rehearsals at the opera house were going smoothly, too, except that Mr. Kavanaugh continued to breeze in from time to time to watch from the back of the theater. It gave Allie the creeps. Janelle continued to stay as far away from Allie and Dub as possible, never even looking in their direction. It made Allie feel very odd, after the conversation she and Janelle had had on the phone. She couldn't help wondering why, exactly, Janelle had called. She appeared to do everything her father wished. Her obedience puzzled Allie. Was it based solely on fear? And, if so, what must it be like to be frightened of your own father?

The secret afternoon rehearsals at Dub's house were a lot more fun. Brad, Joey, Pam, and Julie had all gotten into the spirit of the plan, and each day came up with new ways to make their finale better. Pam and Julie had even agreed to play Skayendady's parents, although they couldn't decide which one would be the father.

Things really started to fall into place when Uncle Hal showed up the Monday before the festival. They were waiting for Pam, who was late, when his van pulled up in Dub's driveway.

"Hi, Uncle Hal!" Brad called.

"Hey, Brad," Uncle Hal called back. He walked over and gave Brad a high five followed by a bear hug. Then he turned to Allie and the others, who were seated on the grass.

"I hear y'all are planning a little surprise," he said cheerfully.

The kids nodded.

"Brad tells me Mr. Darryl Kavanaugh isn't going to be too thrilled about it," Uncle Hal went on.

Oh, no, thought Allie. Uncle Hal was a local businessman. She'd never considered that he might be under Mr. Kavanaugh's thumb, too, along with the town council and a lot of store owners. She hoped he wasn't going to back out.

But Uncle Hal was rubbing his hands together gleefully, making the tattoo on his arm jump. "That big windbag's trying to put me out of business. First he tried to buy me out. The offer he gave me was an insult, and I told him so. So he went to the town council, calling my store a waste of prime real estate. He said it would be better for the town if there were more 'upscale' shops and restaurants there instead of my 'junk shop.' "

Uncle Hal shook his head in disgust. Then he looked around with a wicked grin. "So, if your little plan will get Darryl Kavanaugh's undershorts in a knot, I'm all for it."

Allie laughed in relief.

"When do you want the goods?" Uncle Hal asked.

"The pageant is this Saturday," Dub said. "Can you come back for a dress rehearsal on Thursday?"

Uncle Hal flashed a thumbs-up sign. "You got it. Listen, does that cute director of yours know about this?"

The other kids all glanced uncomfortably at Allie and Dub. "Um, not really," said Dub.

"We thought it was better this way," Allie explained. "If she doesn't know, she can't get into trouble over it."

Uncle Hal nodded, looking thoughtful. "You're probably right. She told me Kavanaugh called her boss on her."

Allie smiled to herself. Uncle Hal and Miss Lunsford had been talking. Maybe they'd even gone on a date. She hoped so.

The kids thanked Uncle Hal. With him on board, Allie began to think they might actually pull off their plan.

Just after Uncle Hal had left, Pam arrived, looking very upset.

"Pam! What's wrong?" Allie asked.

"Karen called me while I was having lunch and asked me all sorts of questions," Pam said. "Either she heard more than we thought when we caught her sneaking around last week, or she's been back. She knows we're planning a new ending for the pageant, and she was fishing around for details. I didn't tell her anything, but she said I'm stupid to hang around with you guys, and we were all going to get into a lot of trouble." Pam stopped and took a deep breath. Allie thought she was trying not to cry. Then she said quietly, "I know I shouldn't let her get to me, but she's so . . . so . . ."

"Reptilian?" Dub suggested. "Viperous? Odious? Despicable?"

The other kids laughed, but Pam looked so forlorn that Allie hastened to reassure her. "But, Pam, you didn't crack! That's great!"

All the kids gave Pam a little cheer, and she smiled weakly.

"But Karen could turn into a real problem," Dub murmured.

"There's no way she's stopping us!" declared Brad.

"Yeah, no way!" Joey shouted.

"We just have to make sure she doesn't find out anything more," Julie added.

Everyone nodded, but Allie wondered if they all shared the same misgivings she was feeling. She couldn't dismiss Karen quite so easily. If Karen wanted to make trouble, she could. And being Karen, she would.

Later that afternoon, Allie and Dub were at the library, looking at pictures of General John Sullivan and George Washington for Joey and Brad to model themselves after.

"We didn't think to ask Uncle Hal for a white wig for Brad," said Dub. "My mom has an old blond one she never wears. I bet she'd let us have it. It's long enough to pull back in a ponytail like George's."

"We could put baby powder on it to make it white," suggested Allie.

They were poring over an encyclopedia as they talked. Allie sensed movement and looked up to see Karen standing before them. Allie tried not to show her dismay. "How long have you been there?" she demanded.

"Long enough," Karen said mysteriously. "Call me crazy, but I don't remember George Washington being in the script I saw . . ." She walked away, glancing back to say, "I told you I'd be watching you."

When she was gone, Allie put her head down on the library table and groaned. "I can't believe it! We are so stupid!"

"Now, wait a second," Dub said. "She can't have been there very long before you saw her. What were we saying, exactly?"

As they tried to reconstruct their conversation, they decided that, besides knowing that George Washington was part of the plan, she couldn't have learned very much. Still, the way things were going, the pageant couldn't come soon enough to suit Allie.

Nineteen

The following afternoon, the kids held their rehearsal in Dub's basement family room to make sure Karen couldn't spy on them. Afterward, Allie and Dub headed for Mrs. Nichols's store on their bikes. Mr. Nichols and Michael were going to come by at closing time so they could all go out for pizza, and then to an early movie. It was only a little after three o'clock, so Allie and Dub were in no particular hurry as they rode their bikes slowly through town.

"Want to stop at Polar Freeze?" Dub asked.

"Sure," said Allie, "if you'll treat. I don't have any money."

"Okay," said Dub.

They were sitting on the bench outside the store licking their cones when Mr. Kavanaugh came walking down the sidewalk toward them.

"Don't look now," Dub began.

"I see him," said Allie. "I guess it's too late to go inside."

"Why should we go inside? It would look like we're scared of him."

Which we are, thought Allie. "Anyway, he sees us now," she said.

Mr. Kavanaugh saw them, all right. He headed directly for their bench and stopped in front of them, his expression tight. He didn't speak, just glared from Allie to Dub and back again.

"Hello, Mr. Kavanaugh," Allie said nervously.

Mr. Kavanaugh didn't return the greeting, but said abruptly, "Didn't I make myself clear when I caught you out at Poplar Point?"

Allie remained silent. Dub said, "I'm not sure what you mean."

"I've had a phone call from someone who said that you two are still trying to meddle in affairs that are none of your concern, namely my pageant. I had hoped you were smarter than that."

Allie asked indignantly, "Who is this person?"

"Someone who wants to do what's best for this town," Mr. Kavanaugh said. "Which is a concept you two are having trouble grasping. So let me spell it out for you one more time. The pageant and the hotel project will go on as planned. And two kids, both of whose parents depend upon me for their businesses, would be wise to drop any silly ideas they have about interfering. *Now* do we understand each other?"

Neither Allie nor Dub answered. Mr. Kavanaugh nodded and said, "Good."

Allie and Dub watched as he strode casually up the street and disappeared into the bank. Allie shivered, and it wasn't from the mint chip ice cream she'd eaten.

"Is it my imagination," Dub said, "or were we just given a warning?"

Twenty

Stunned by Mr. Kavanaugh's comments, Allie and Dub remained on the bench outside Polar Freeze, trying to decide what to do. There had been a real threat beneath the surface of Mr. Kavanaugh's words; they'd both felt it.

"Do you think it was Karen who called him?" Allie asked Dub.

"It would take a lot of nerve, but she's got plenty of that."

"She doesn't know what we're planning to do," Allie said, "so how could she tell him?"

"She probably made some vague remarks about how we were up to something with his play," Dub said darkly. "Typical Karen. Who needs the facts to stir up trouble?" He snorted. "And he believes she's doing it because she cares about what's 'best for the town.' That's a laugh."

"If he knew for sure what we were doing, he'd have said so, right?" Allie asked. "So he's warning us not to do *anything* that might mess up his plans."

"I guess so," said Dub.

"But he made it sound like if we do something he doesn't like, we'll hurt our parents' businesses," Allie said in a small voice. "I'd feel awful if my mom had to close her store, or if your parents went out of business or something, all because of us."

"He can't really do that," Dub said scornfully. "Uncle Hal called him a big windbag. He's just shooting his mouth off, thinking he can scare us because we're kids."

Allie had a momentary image of Skayendady's tearstained face. After several relatively carefree days, the burden of being a ghost magnet was beginning to feel heavy again.

"We could come up with another plan," she said, though she couldn't imagine what that might be.

Dub looked at her. "Yeah, *right*. Like what? The pageant's just four days away."

They talked until it was time to meet Allie's family at the store, and decided that they weren't going to let Darryl Kavanaugh intimidate them into abandoning their plan.

When they were settled in a booth at Papa Gino's pizza parlor along with Michael and Allie's parents, Allie tried to hold on to the bravado she and Dub had managed to muster. After the waitress had taken their orders and brought them bread and drinks, Michael told about his day with Fritzi. Listening to Michael and watching his bright, animated face, Allie had a sudden idea. It was sure to make their surprise ending to the pageant even more effective.

"Hey, Mike!" she said excitedly when he'd finished his story. "How would you like to be in the pageant with Dub and me? In a battle scene?"

Dub looked at her, a curious expression on his face.

"I thought the play was for kids your age," Mrs. Nichols interjected.

"Well, yeah, it is," Allie answered. "But there's a four-year-old boy in the final scene. I was just thinking how much more realistic it would be to have a real four-year-old onstage to play my brother."

"Yeah!" Michael exclaimed loudly. " 'Cause *I'm* four. And I *am* your brother! Can I, Mom?"

Mrs. Nichols said, "Have you discussed this with the director, Allie?"

"Not yet," Allie admitted.

"If she says it's okay, it's all right with me. But you need to talk to her."

"Okay," said Allie.

Dub looked worried, and Allie knew he was wondering how she could ask Miss Lunsford about Michael when the director didn't even know about the final scene they were planning. Allie didn't know herself. She only knew that Michael's presence on the stage would make their surprise ending much, much stronger.

"I should probably warn you guys," Allie said to her parents. "The four-year-old boy dies at the end."

"Goodness!" Mrs. Nichols said. "I don't think I'm going to like watching that."

"I die, too, Mom," Allie informed her.

"Oh, dear," said Mrs. Nichols, looking distressed.

"Mom," said Michael, "it's not real, just pretend."

"Oh, well then," Mrs. Nichols said. "I guess that's okay."

Dub turned to Michael and said quietly, "Don't get your hopes up too much, Mike. First we have to find out if it's okay with the lady who runs the show."

"We'll talk to her tomorrow," Allie promised.

Dub gave her a look that said, *How do you think you're going to pull this off?*

Allie wished she knew.

Twenty-one

The next morning, Allie and Dub met early to plan how they might approach Miss Lunsford at rehearsal.

"I wish you'd worked this out with her before you mentioned it to Michael," Dub said.

"I know," Allie said with a sigh. "I guess I got carried away."

"Well," Dub said halfheartedly, "Miss Lunsford is always talking about improvising."

"Dub, Mr. Kavanaugh bullied Miss Lunsford into giving Janelle my part," Allie said. "He basically threatened her, just the way he did us yesterday. I bet she doesn't like him any more than we do."

"Probably not," Dub replied. "But she doesn't want to lose her job, either."

"She was mad, though," Allie said. "I could tell. And she told me the reason she went along with it was so Mr. Kavanaugh didn't cancel the whole pag-

eant. She didn't want people to be disappointed."
Allie grinned slyly at Dub. "Maybe she wouldn't
mind if Mr. Kavanaugh is 'disappointed' in front of
everybody in town."

Dub shrugged. "I guess all we can do is ask and
see what she says."

But to their dismay, when they arrived at the
opera house Karen Laver was already marching in
through the front door, her chin raised high in determination.

"Oh, no," Allie moaned.

"She must have decided Miss Lunsford needed to
hear about her concern for the good of the town,"
Dub said grimly.

"She's going to ruin our chance," Allie said.
"Come on. Let's see if we can listen."

"We're getting as bad as Karen, eavesdropping all
the time," Dub said.

"We're just fighting fire with fire," Allie replied
with a shrug. "Come on."

They quickly stashed their bikes and crept into the
lobby, stopping at one of the two arched entrances
to the auditorium. Peeking around the corner, they
saw Karen standing before Miss Lunsford, a smug
smile on her face. Her cheeks were pink with excitement as she said eagerly, "Miss Lunsford, there's
something I really think you should know about the
pageant."

Miss Lunsford said, "Oh? And what's that, Karen?"

"Well," Karen began, "I just happened to overhear some of your cast members talking and—"

Allie elbowed Dub and whispered in outrage, " 'Just happened to overhear'! What a liar!"

Karen dropped her voice then and continued talking in conspiratorial tones. Allie and Dub caught their own names from time to time, but not much else. Miss Lunsford's face remained impassive, and it was impossible to see how she was reacting to the news.

When Karen had finished, Miss Lunsford said calmly, "Is that everything you wanted to tell me?"

Karen nodded.

"Very well," said Miss Lunsford. "Thank you, Karen. I'll take care of it."

Karen asked eagerly, "Are they in trouble?"

"I don't think you need to involve yourself with that," Miss Lunsford replied. "And I think it would be best if you didn't mention this to anyone else," Miss Lunsford said.

"What are you going to do?" Karen asked, obviously reluctant to leave without knowing the details.

But Miss Lunsford wasn't playing. "Thank you for coming, Karen. Now, if that's all, you may be on your way. You did tell me how busy you are this summer, didn't you? And the cast will be arriving any moment."

Karen walked back up the aisle to the lobby, a look of discontent on her face. Allie and Dub quickly hid in the shadows behind the popcorn machine. When she was gone, Dub said, "The jig's up. We might as well go face the music."

"Yeah," said Allie, her voice glum. "Let's get it over with."

Without a word they trudged to the front of the theater, where Miss Lunsford was sitting in the first row. She appeared lost in thought, and didn't notice them right away. When she looked up, her eyes widened with surprise.

There was an awkward silence. "Uh, Miss Lunsford," Allie began. "There's something we have to tell you. See, we found out what really happened at Pop—"

But, to her surprise, Miss Lunsford interrupted to say, "And there's something *I'd* like to tell *you*. It's my feeling that the pageant is coming together quite nicely, except for the ending, which I think needs a little work, don't you?"

Dumbly, Allie and Dub nodded.

"So I'm delighted to hear that you have embraced the idea of improvising," she went on. "You know my position on that. It keeps things fresh. And even directors enjoy surprises." She looked at them pointedly, a funny, crooked smile playing about the corners of her mouth.

Allie blinked, too taken aback for the moment to respond. Then she gathered her wits and asked, "One of our, um, improvisations might possibly involve having a real four-year-old boy play Skayendady's little brother. I was just wondering if that would be okay."

"Interesting idea," said Miss Lunsford, nodding with approval. Then she held up both hands, palms out. "Don't tell me any more. Surprise me."

Allie smiled. "Okay."

Some of the other cast members arrived, and Miss Lunsford stood up. In a low voice she said, "For now, I think it's best if I know nothing more about this. But if there's anything I can do to help out the night of the production, you let me know." She waved to the kids who were coming down the aisle, and moved to speak to them.

Allie and Dub looked at each other in wonder. "I can't believe it!" Allie said after a moment.

"Me neither," said Dub. Then he added slowly, "You know, I think Karen may have actually done us a favor by telling on us."

"It would kill her to know that," Allie said dryly.

Dub grinned. "Then I may just have to tell her."

Twenty-two

With only two more days before the festival on Saturday, Allie and the rest of the cast were becoming excited—and nervous. At the Whitwells' house that Thursday afternoon, Michael joined Allie, Dub, Brad, Joey, Julie, and Pam to run through the new ending from start to finish, just as if it were the real thing.

While they waited for Uncle Hal to show up with the promised costumes and props, they admired Brad in his outfit. Wearing Dub's mother's blond wig dusted with baby powder, with the ends tied back in a little ponytail, he looked a lot like Washington. The rest of his costume consisted of a white shirt, to which Allie had added frilly lace at the neck, and a satin vest. Mrs. Nichols had provided a pair of knee-high boots for him to tuck his pants into.

In their research at the library, Allie and Dub had

found letters and speeches given by Cornplanter, George Washington, and General Sullivan. Dub, Brad, and Joey were going to use portions of their characters' actual words. Allie was a little worried, not about Dub and Brad so much, but about Joey, who hadn't realized when he took the part that memorization was going to be required. He was complaining, "Man, this is too much like school," when the doorbell rang. They opened the door to Uncle Hal.

He pointed to the driveway, where the van was parked, the rear doors flung open. "Come check out my wares," he said.

They all ran out to the driveway, where Uncle Hal pulled out piles of old-fashioned-looking military jackets and pants in shades of blue and gray and brown, some with epaulets and shiny buttons. He held up a brass trumpet, which Joey immediately seized.

"Cool! I can use this to lead the charge!" he cried, and blew a series of piercing blasts.

Uncle Hal had brought military hats of all sorts, too, and in short order the soldiers were dressed. At first Michael was disappointed not to be able to wear a uniform, but he forgot all about clothing when Uncle Hal brought out the "guns." Allie thought her little brother's eyes would bug out of his head as Uncle Hal demonstrated how to use the starter pistols. To Allie they sounded real.

"Okay, now," Uncle Hal said, "you said you needed smoke bombs."

"Yeah," Dub said eagerly. "Did you bring some?"

The kids all crowded closer to look.

"After careful consideration, I decided to bring the grenade-style units," Uncle Hal said, holding up a little canister.

"*Grenade* style!" Joey repeated happily. "Cool!"

"See, you just pull the pin here," Uncle Hal explained. "You don't have to mess with a match. You're not going to believe how much smoke these babies give off."

He held the grenade out and said to Michael, "You want to pull the pin, little buddy?"

Michael nodded eagerly.

"Wait, Uncle Hal, are you sure it's safe?" Allie asked.

"This here's a nonexplosive, nontoxic model. See the label? Says they're for use in 'theatrical productions,' which is what you've got here, plus in magic shows, police drills, and what have you," said Uncle Hal. "They're perfectly safe. No way I'd endanger my little buddy here," he added with a wink at Michael. "Go ahead. Just tug on that pin right there and toss it onto the grass."

Michael stepped forward, pulled the pin, and jumped back with a shriek of delight. Soon a thick cloud of white smoke filled the air.

"Wow!" said Dub.

"Cool!" cried Brad.

For once, Joey was speechless.

Michael tugged on Allie's hand. "Allie! Look!"

Allie, too, was amazed. It was quite an impressive display. She watched the smoke thin out and disperse in the light breeze. But, she thought uneasily, the pageant was going to take place inside, not outside on Dub's lawn. She pictured the smoke filling the opera house, imagined people panicking, thinking there was a fire.

"Um, Uncle Hal," she began, "the pageant's inside, at the opera house downtown. Is that going to be a problem, do you think?"

Uncle Hal frowned for a moment. Then he brightened. "Tell you what. Is there a back door to the stage area?"

Allie glanced at the others, and they nodded.

"Good. Make sure that door is open for ventilation. Do you think you can get me backstage?"

"I don't see why not," said Allie.

"Great. I'll take care of setting off the smoke bomb, and I'll rig up a fan that'll blow the smoke away from the audience and toward the door. We'll only need to set off one of these puppies, anyhow. You'll get a nice, smoky effect and the nervous Nellies in the audience won't be having heart palpitations. How's that sound?"

"It sounds terrific," Allie said, relieved at the idea of Uncle Hal being on hand.

Uncle Hal smiled at them all. "So. Looks like you're set. Can you think of anything else before I take off?"

There was one detail that had been bothering Allie, and it came to her that Uncle Hal might be just the person to deal with it. "We need somebody to work the spotlights," she said hesitantly. "Do you think—"

"You got it," Uncle Hal said confidently.

Allie thanked him and he turned to climb into the van, saying, "You call if you need anything else, okay?"

"Okay," said Brad. "Thanks a lot, Uncle Hal."

As the other kids were saying their thanks, Michael ran forward and hugged Uncle Hal.

Uncle Hal gave him a wink. "See you Saturday, little buddy."

Allie smiled. "Looks like somebody has a new hero," she murmured to Dub.

"He's not the only one," Dub said with a grin. "Uncle Hal is awesome. Thanks to him, we are going to blow the audience away!"

Allie laughed and said, only half-kidding, "That's what I'm afraid of."

Twenty-three

On Saturday, Allie and her family arrived at the lakefront park, where the festival was already in full swing. Mr. and Mrs. Nichols were taking Michael on the kiddie rides, and Allie was meeting up with Dub. The plan was for Allie's parents to take Michael home for an afternoon nap so he'd make it through the pageant. Allie and Dub would stay all day at the festival, eating both lunch and dinner there.

For several hours, they went on their favorite rides, then took a break for some food. They were meandering around eating cotton candy when they saw the familiar figure of their sixth-grade teacher, accompanied by his golden retriever.

"Hi, Mr. Henry!" they called.

Allie bent down to pet Hoover, saying, "You're

looking quite sporty today, Hoovey, in your red bandanna."

"She felt the occasion required something festive," Mr. Henry explained.

Allie asked, "You're coming to the pageant tonight, right, Mr. Henry?"

"Absolutely," he said. "Half of my last class is in it, I hear."

With a little smile at Dub, Allie said, "Be sure to stay until the very end."

"Yeah!" Dub said. "Don't leave early, even if you think the beginning is kind of boring."

"Because the ending is important," Allie added.

Mr. Henry nodded. "I was planning on staying to the end, anyway," he said. "But now you can be sure I will. Why do I have the funny feeling you guys are up to something?" He looked from one to the other, a question in his eyes.

Allie and Dub gave him their most innocent expressions, and he laughed.

"I remember once when we were all complaining about something we were doing in social studies, you said the reason we study history is so we can learn from the mistakes of the past," Dub said, his tone serious.

Mr. Henry looked impressed. "It's nice to know someone was listening," he said.

"Umm, you might need to bring that up in our defense," Dub went on.

"Your defense? Now you've really got me intrigued."

After they'd said goodbye to Mr. Henry and Hoover, Allie and Dub headed over to the craft booths, only to run smack into Karen Laver. "I heard Miss Lunsford found out somehow about your little surprise," she said. "That's too bad. I hope you didn't get into too much trouble."

"As a matter of fact, we didn't get into trouble at all," Allie said breezily. "Must be Miss Lunsford didn't think that information came from a very reliable source."

Karen's confident expression faltered for a moment, then her usual smirk returned. "Well, Miss Lunsford is a pathetic wimp. But there's someone else who I think will appreciate hearing all about the latest detail I've learned."

"Oh, yeah?" Allie said recklessly. "Who?"

"Mr. Kavanaugh. You've heard of him, I'm sure." Karen gave Allie a malicious grin and added, "Somehow I don't think he's going to be too thrilled to hear about the *smoke bombs*."

At that, Allie felt all her bravado drain away. In their eagerness to see Uncle Hal's goodies, they had forgotten to make sure the coast was clear outside

Dub's house. "You—you're not going to tell him," she said feebly.

"Oh, no? Just watch me." Karen's face was flushed with triumph. "I'm sure he's around here somewhere. And if I don't see him here, he'll be at the pageant." She gave them a little wiggle of her fingers. "Ta-ta, now."

Stricken, Allie looked at Dub. "She saw us set off the smoke bomb."

"We're toast," he said.

"What time is it?" Allie asked Dub.

"Almost five," he said. "We have to be at the opera house at six. We have an hour to . . . what? Keep Karen away from Mr. Kavanaugh? Lure him away somewhere so Karen can't find him? Or, I know! We catch up with Karen and, by appealing to her better nature, get her to keep quiet!"

"Hah," said Allie in a dull voice.

Dub sighed. "It's hopeless. She's right, she can always tell him at the pageant."

Nevertheless, they spent the next hour searching the crowd in vain for either Karen or the Kavanaughs. At five minutes to six, there was nothing to do but go to the opera house and hope for a miracle.

Twenty-four

Despite her worries about Karen Laver and the Kavanaughs, Allie was immediately swept up in the chaos and excitement backstage at the opera house. The cast members were getting dressed, practicing their lines, and proclaiming dramatically about how nervous they were.

"They think *they're* nervous," Dub whispered. "What about us?"

Allie's parents arrived, bringing Michael, whose entire body seemed to be vibrating with excitement.

"Hey, you look great, Mike!" said Allie.

Michael stood, proudly displaying his outfit. He was shirtless. Over his shorts he had on a leather breechcloth Mrs. Nichols had made, tied on with a beaded sash. On his feet were moccasins, and around his neck he wore some strings of colorful beads. He was holding his father's old wooden lacrosse stick with leather laces, which Mr. Nichols had cut short to four-year-old size.

"You gotta get dressed, too, Allie," he said with concern.

"I will," Allie assured him.

"Michael, we're going to leave you here with Allie and Dub, and get some seats right up front," said Mr. Nichols. "Are you all set?"

Michael nodded. His parents hugged him, then Allie, and Dub, too. "Good luck!" they said as they left the backstage area.

When Allie and Dub were dressed, they joined Pam and Julie, who were peering out from behind the curtain at the crowd that was already beginning to pour into the theater.

"Have you seen Karen?" Allie asked urgently.

"No. And where's Uncle Hal, I wonder?" asked Julie.

"He's going to wait until the pageant starts, then sneak back here," said Dub. "Just so nobody gets suspicious about what he's doing."

Allie peered past the curtain to look for Karen and saw the Kavanaughs take seats in the front row.

"Oh, no!" Julie said. "The Kavanaughs are going to sit right under our noses! I think I'm going to have a heart attack."

"Don't look at them," Dub advised.

Allie watched as her parents approached the front

row and prepared to take two of the open seats. Dub's parents arrived at the same moment and greeted Mr. and Mrs. Nichols. It looked as if they were going to sit together when Mr. Kavanaugh went over to them, smiled, spoke, and gestured to the entire front row in the center section. Allie couldn't hear him, but it was obvious that he was claiming those seats for himself.

"I can't believe it!" Allie said, outraged. "Look at him, hogging all the best seats for himself and his friends."

"He has friends?" Dub asked. He and the other kids peered through the curtain again to watch as Dub's and Allie's parents were directed to the second row, while Mr. Kavanaugh, all smiles, called to some other people and motioned them toward the front. Mrs. Kavanaugh was seated, looking down at her lap. Allie remembered Janelle saying that her parents had fought about the pageant and that her father had, naturally, won.

"Man," said Dub, watching Mr. Kavanaugh with disdain. "He acts like he owns the place."

"He probably does," said Julie. She scanned the crowd, looked at her watch, and said, "My parents better get here soon, or they're going to be way in the back."

"Hey, I didn't know Indians had pink plastic digital watches back then," Pam said innocently.

"Oops!" said Julie. She took off her watch and put it in the pocket of her calico dress. "That was a close one."

Just then Allie spotted Karen Laver coming down the aisle toward the front row. She gasped, and elbowed Dub sharply. "Look! It's Karen—and she's heading for the Kavanaughs."

With a simpering smile on her face, Karen stood waiting for the Kavanaughs to finish their conversation.

Miss Lunsford bustled past backstage, her cheeks flushed, calling, "Two minutes until curtain! Places, everyone. Places, please!"

Allie and the other kids couldn't tear their eyes away as the Kavanaughs turned to look questioningly at Karen. Allie's heart sank when Karen began to speak. She watched Mr. and Mrs. Kavanaugh's expressions change from polite interest to surprise. When Karen had finished, Mrs. Kavanaugh's face was unreadable. But there was no mistaking her husband's fury.

The house lights went dark, and Allie and the others ran to take their places as the curtain rose.

Twenty-five

In the first scene of the pageant, Allie stood onstage as Janelle Kavanaugh spoke the opening words. "My name is Skayendady. I am a Seneca Indian. My age is twelve winters. I belong to the Wolf Clan."

Allie tried to collect herself, thankful for the moment that she was blinded by the bright stage lights, as Janelle went on with the words of the script: "This is my story. It is a story of how settlers from across the sea came to the lands of my people. It is a story of friendship."

Janelle had never become comfortable in her role. Her delivery was, if possible, more flat and unconvincing than ever. *Maybe because she knows it's all untrue,* Allie thought.

Allie went through the motions of her part, acting out the scenes where she and the other Senecas first greeted the settlers, accepted their gifts, and gave them food in return. It seemed to drag on and on, and felt more false than ever. She was grateful, though, for all the rehearsals that allowed her to keep going even though her mind was spinning in panic about Mr. Kavanaugh.

Finally, there was a scene that didn't include her, and she was able to leave the stage. She passed Dub, who was just coming on. There was no time to talk, but he gave her a wide-eyed look and mouthed the words *Mr. Kavanaugh!*

From offstage, Allie peered around the edge of the curtain and saw that Mr. Kavanaugh was no longer in his seat. He was standing between a set of stairs that led up to the stage and a doorway that led to the backstage right area. His face was tight and angry.

"Allie!" someone whispered. It was Michael, standing next to Brad and Joey. He was grinning, completely unaware of the impending disaster. Even in her desperate state, Allie noted that Brad and Joey looked terrific, every inch the figures of George Washington and General John Sullivan.

"Hi, Mike," she said hurriedly. "Hi, guys. Boy, am I glad you're here. Mr. Kavanaugh—"

"We know," said Brad. "Dub told us. What are we going to do?"

"I don't know," said Allie. "Where's Uncle Hal?"

"Checking out the spotlight system one last time," said Brad.

"What if Kavanaugh just barges up onstage before our part even gets started?" Joey asked.

Allie, too, was worried about this.

Miss Lunsford rushed by then, looking frazzled. "Allie!" she said. "You're on in the next scene!"

"Okay," Allie answered. To Brad and Joey she said, "Look, I've got to get back out there. Just go ahead with the plan, I guess. And keep your fingers crossed!"

They nodded, but Michael grasped her hand, his face grave, and asked, "When do we get to do the smoke bombs?"

She knelt down in front of him, took his other hand, and tried to smile. "Soon, Mike," she said. "You stay with these guys until it's time, then do everything just the way we practiced, okay?"

Michael nodded, and smiled, too. "Okay!"

Allie raced back to take her place for the scene in which the settlers and the Seneca gather for a feast. As she pretended to be enjoying the wonderful food and her newfound friendship with the settlers, she looked over at Mr. Kavanaugh, who was still standing by the stage door. Immediately she wished she hadn't.

The thin mask of joviality and charm he usually remembered to wear had been completely stripped away, revealing his true face. He was staring back at her, and she thought that the anger he'd shown before was far less frightening than this cold appraisal. She saw clearly that, at that moment, she was no more to him than an obstacle in his path. She was an annoying bug that needed to be squashed. He was simply figuring out the least troublesome, most efficient way to go about it.

To add to the tumult in her mind, she was strongly aware of the presence of the ghost of the real Skayendady. For over a week, Skayendady's spirit had been hovering in the background, seemingly content with the way Allie was handling matters. She hadn't done anything—or made Allie do anything—overt or embarrassing. But now Allie sensed that she was greatly agitated.

At last the feast scene ended. As the curtain was closing, she saw Mr. Kavanaugh reach into his pocket and take out what looked like a cell phone. Allie fled the stage.

The next scene was a long one in which the Seneca braves showed their hunting and fishing methods to the male settlers. Allie felt utterly unnerved. She really needed to talk to Dub.

Miss Lunsford, the techs, and the cast members who weren't onstage gathered in the backstage left area, but Allie headed to the quiet, shadowy wing to the right, where there was a little area partitioned off with plywood that had been painted black. She had last seen Dub there, pacing back and forth, going over the lines of his big scene one final time.

"Dub!" she whispered. She heard muffled footsteps and whispered again, "Dub? I've got to talk to you!"

Allie peered around the plywood partition into the dimness, where music stands, folding chairs, some risers, an electric keyboard, and bits of stage sets and scenery from past productions were jumbled together haphazardly.

A creak was followed by a faint click, as if the door that led from the theater to the backstage area was being closed very carefully. Then Allie heard more footsteps, coming toward her.

Uncertain now and a little nervous, she whispered, "Dub, what are you doing?"

A figure stepped from the shadows. "Dub—" Allie began. Then her stomach flip-flopped. It wasn't Dub but Darryl Kavanaugh.

Twenty-six

For a moment Allie and Darryl Kavanaugh stared at each other in silence. Then Mr. Kavanaugh spoke. In a low voice, so as not to be heard from the theater, he said, "Call it off."

Allie was too stunned to respond.

"You know what I'm talking about. Call it off now."

When Allie still didn't answer, he sighed and said, "You've stepped into something way over your head. I know all about this crazy stunt of yours, and it isn't going to work. So save yourself a lot of embarrassment and stop it now." The softness of his voice only added to the menace Allie felt in his words.

"Go tell your friends," he said calmly. "The fun's over."

Allie wanted to speak or run or do *something*, but she felt immobilized. She knew that all she had to do was scream, and everyone in the theater would hear her. But she didn't want to ruin the pageant, not now, when they were so close to the end.

Her mind raced. If Mr. Kavanaugh was sure their "stunt" wouldn't work, why was he trying to get Allie to call it off? Maybe there was still a chance they would succeed.

"No," she said quietly.

Darryl Kavanaugh dropped his calm demeanor and let out an irritated sigh. "Listen, you little brat," he said venomously. "I'm trying to give you a chance here, but I've had it with you."

Allie felt her heart slamming in her chest as Darryl Kavanaugh shook his head with disgust and walked toward her. He reached out and grabbed her upper arms so tightly that it hurt.

"Oww!" she said.

Mr. Kavanaugh brought his face to within inches of hers and spoke slowly. "You call this off *now*, or, believe me, you're going to be very, very sorry."

Allie stifled the scream that rose in her throat. Just then a small frightened voice cried, "Allie!"

Mr. Kavanaugh looked up in surprise and loosened his grasp on her. Allie turned to see Michael watching wide-eyed, his little lacrosse stick raised in alarm.

"Mike, go! Get Uncle Hal!" she gasped.

But instead of turning around, Michael charged

forward. "You let go of Allie!" he said fiercely. He drew back his lacrosse stick and, before Allie could take in what was happening, he whacked Mr. Kavanaugh in the side with it. Mr. Kavanaugh stumbled and fell backward against a set of risers, which were piled high with a miscellaneous assortment of stored items. A speaker the size of a small refrigerator teetered and, in what seemed like slow motion, fell, hitting him on the side of the head before landing with a loud thud.

Allie watched in horrified fascination as Mr. Kavanaugh fell to the floor, where he lay with his mouth hanging open, still and quiet as a stone. *Oh, no,* she thought. *Please don't let him be dead!*

Michael ran over and they both knelt beside the prostrate man. Michael looked at Allie, his face white and his eyes wide with shock. With a sob of relief, Allie saw Mr. Kavanaugh's chest rise and fall. "He's breathing, Mike. He's okay. I mean, he's alive, anyway." Her mind raced and she added, "Quick! Run and find Uncle Hal!"

She kept her eyes on the front of Mr. Kavanaugh's shirt, holding panic at bay by focusing on every breath he took.

Soon Michael came running back with Uncle Hal right behind him.

"He was hurting Allie!" Michael said, pointing to Darryl Kavanaugh. "I hit him with my lacrosse stick and he fell and that big black thing fell on his head!"

"Did he hurt you, Allie?" Uncle Hal asked, his eyes blazing with anger.

"Yes, but Michael stopped him." She didn't add how terrified she had felt. She looked at the still form of Mr. Kavanaugh. "What should we do?" she asked shakily.

"You go back to your play, and let me take care of him," said Uncle Hal. "I'll call for an ambulance, just to be sure, but I guarantee you he's got a hard head."

"What if he wakes up?" Allie asked.

Uncle Hal grinned. "I've got something out in my van that will keep him from causing any more trouble."

"What is it?" Allie asked curiously.

"Uncle Hal never reveals his secret methods," he said, giving Michael a little wink.

Miss Lunsford rushed up then, looking even more frazzled than before. *"Allie!"* she said urgently. "There you are! What on earth is going on over here? You're making much too much noise! Cornplanter is about to go on for his speech—you've got to get over there right away!" She looked past Allie, saw Mr. Kavanaugh, and gasped.

"Go," Uncle Hal urged Allie. He cocked a thumb at Mr. Kavanaugh. "I'll take care of him."

"Michael, you come with us," Allie said, grabbing

his hand and running over to where Miss Lunsford stood waiting anxiously.

"What happened to Mr. Kav—" Miss Lunsford began. Then she stopped and said breathlessly, "Oh, never mind, you'll have to tell me later—"

She broke off as they saw Janelle stepping out from behind the curtain onto the stage. They heard her announce, "The pageant will now end with a speech by Cornplanter, the legendary Seneca orator."

This was the moment when the surprise ending was supposed to begin. Dub was going to give a speech, all right, but not the one Mrs. Kavanaugh had written for him.

Allie gave Dub a quick high five before he stepped out into the spotlight. She wished she could watch him, but she had work to do. While Dub was speaking, Allie, Julie, and Pam had to pull off the trickiest part of their plan, the part they couldn't rehearse in advance. They had to explain about the surprise ending to the cast members who didn't know a thing about it, and get them on board. Their speedy cooperation was essential; without it, the plan was doomed.

As Allie, Julie, and Pam were trying to assemble the cast backstage, Miss Lunsford came to their rescue. The kids quickly gathered at her direction.

Speaking in a low voice so as not to be heard by

the audience, Miss Lunsford said, "Things onstage are about to take an unexpected turn. We're going to be adding a final scene that we never rehearsed. Remember when we talked about improvisation? Well, now is your chance to be part of the magic of live theater. Allie?"

Allie gave her a grateful smile and quickly explained how the massacre would unfold onstage, and that she would be playing Skayendady in the scene. "So," she finished, "who wants to help?"

"The more soldiers and Indians out there, the better," Miss Lunsford urged.

Allie had been afraid some of the kids might be fearful or resistant, but, after their initial surprise, they all appeared enthusiastic about the idea. To Allie's relief, they were staring at her eagerly, asking what they should do.

All except Janelle, who was standing stock-still, her face white, her eyes wide with shock.

Allie looked away quickly and continued talking. "Okay," she said. "If you're already dressed as an Indian, you'll be part of a scene where we're peacefully going about our business in the village. When the soldiers show up and start shooting, scream, cry, fall down, pretend to die—you get the idea."

"Cool!" said the other kids.

"But no fooling around. This was serious business," Allie warned. "Okay, so the rest of you will be soldiers," she went on, pointing to a pile of military clothing supplied by Uncle Hal. "If you want to be one of the army guys, put on some soldier stuff. Julie and Pam will help you. Grab torches"—she indicated a pile of sticks with tongues of orange and red and yellow cellophane taped to the ends—"and guns."

"Guns?" one of the boys asked excitedly.

"They're not real," Allie told him. "But when you fire them, they're going to sound real. Oh, and there's going to be a lot of smoke, too, so don't freak."

Miss Lunsford added, "We need to do this very quickly and very quietly, people. Soldiers, don't worry about how well your costume fits. With all the smoke and all the action, the audience isn't going to notice."

There were murmurs of "Wow," and "Cool!" as the cast members scurried to get ready.

"Thanks so much, Miss Lunsford," Allie said.

Miss Lunsford grinned. "My pleasure," she answered.

Allie smiled back, then turned to find herself face-to-face with Janelle. She caught her breath. The two girls stared at each other for what felt like a very long time.

Allie's mind was spinning in dismay. She and the others had come so close. And now, at the last moment, Janelle was going to ruin everything.

Instead, to Allie's amazement, Janelle removed Skayendady's beaded headpiece. "Here," she said. "You're going to need this, right?"

It took Allie a moment to take in what Janelle was doing. She was so overwhelmed with surprise and relief and gratitude, she didn't know what to say. Impulsively, she reached over and hugged the other girl.

Then Janelle said hesitantly, "Do you think I can be a soldier?"

Allie looked at her. "Sure," she said. "There are plenty of costumes."

"I just pretend to kill people, right?" Janelle asked.

Allie nodded. Then she asked quietly, "Are you sure you want to do this? Your father—"

For a moment, doubt and fear flashed across Janelle's face. Then she straightened her shoulders and interrupted Allie. "I'm sure."

Twenty-seven

Allie ran to the edge of the stage and peered past the curtain to watch as Dub, dressed in the traditional feathered headgear, bib, leggings, and breechcloth of the Seneca male, paused for a moment in his speech. Then, with his chin held high, he continued speaking in a commanding voice. "Perhaps such scenes as you have just viewed did, indeed, take place between my people and yours. But now I wish you to know the truth about what happened on September 8, 1779, to the Seneca village at what you now call Poplar Point.

"At the time of your Revolutionary War, my people and the five other nations of the Iroquois Confederacy were forced to choose sides in a war we could not truly understand. The red-coated soldiers called us their brothers and said that the Great King in England considered us his children. They told us that their king had power no people could resist and that his goodness was as bright as the sun. What they said went to our hearts; we promised to obey this king. What the Seneca nation promises, we faithfully perform.

"But General George Washington, commander of the colonial troops, vowed revenge on us for siding with the British. He chose General John Sullivan to mount a campaign to punish us."

The spotlight on Dub faded, and another shone on Brad.

Brad, resplendent as George Washington, sat at a desk drafting a letter. When he finished writing, he picked up the letter and read it aloud.

"Orders of George Washington to General John Sullivan, at Headquarters, May 31, 1779.

"The Expedition you are appointed to command is to be directed against the hostile tribes of the Six Nations of Indians, with their associates and adherents. The immediate objects are the total destruction and devastation of their settlements, and the capture of as many prisoners of every age and sex as possible. It will be essential to ruin their crops now in the ground and prevent their planting more.

"I would recommend that troops be detached to lay waste all the settlements around, with instructions to do it in the most effectual manner, that the country may not be merely overrun, but destroyed. Accept no offer of peace before the total ruin of their settlements is effected."

Then the spotlight returned to Cornplanter, who spoke to George Washington: "You say we are in your hand and that by closing it you will crush us to nothing. Are you determined to crush us?

"Before you determine on a measure so unjust, look up to God, who made us as well as you. We hope he will not permit you to destroy the whole of our nation. Great Chief Washington, we open our hearts to you. Hear us once more."

The spotlight returned to George Washington, who shook his head, picked up the pen again, and put his signature on the order to General Sullivan.

Next, a spotlight shone on Joey, attired in the military uniform of General John Sullivan. He looked up from the letter he was reading and said, "I, General John Sullivan, received my orders from General Washington. My men and I traveled through the territory of the Six Nations, systematically carrying out our mission in one Indian village after another. On September 8, 1779, my troops and I were camped on the east side of Seneca Lake. From there, I spotted a prosperous village across the water on the west side, at what you now call Poplar Point. I ordered it destroyed. My army descended upon the village and burned twenty dwellings there. They burned the fields of corn, peas, beans, melons, cucumbers, and potatoes, and the orchards of apples and peaches. They killed hogs, fowl, and horses. They killed the men, women, and children."

At that moment, the stage was plunged into darkness.

Then, under dim lights, Skayendady and the other Seneca Indians took their places. As she played her role, Allie imagined being in the audience watching the scene unfold:

Skayendady joined the other women and girls, who were laughing and chatting, scraping hides, doing beadwork, hoeing the gardens, tending to their cooking fires, and soothing their babies. The warriors and hunters sat talking and joking in the peaceful morning.

A very young boy came onto the stage, smiled at Skayendady, and waved. He began to toss a lacrosse ball into the air and catch it in his stick.

Suddenly the clip-clop of many horses galloping filled the air. A trumpet sounded. Skayendady and the others, startled, looked up from their work and play. A shot rang out, then another, then many more. Several of the women fell to the ground.

Terrified screams tore through the air. Horses whinnied as soldiers surged onto the stage, firing their guns in deafening blasts. Some of them held torches. Smoke filled the stage as they set fire to buildings and plants and trees.

Warriors were shot before they could rise from their places on the ground to find their own weapons. Women and children fled, panicking, in all directions.

The young boy ran toward a soldier who was setting fire to a house. The boy brought his lacrosse stick back over his shoulder, but before he could strike the soldier who was burning his home, another soldier raised his gun, aimed, and fired. The boy's lacrosse stick fell from his hands as he crumpled to the ground.

Skayendady ran to the boy and fell to her knees beside him, cradling his head in her arms. A moan rose from her throat, grew louder, and became a keening wail. A man and a woman, choking from the smoke, tried to make their way through the chaos and confusion to their weeping daughter and lifeless son, and were cut down in midstride. Skayendady, seeing this, let out a last heartbroken cry before she, too, was shot. She died, her little brother in her arms.

Smoke drifted in wispy ribbons over the motionless bodies of the slain. There was no sound at all then except for the final moans of agony from the dying.

After a moment, General Sullivan stepped onto the stage, surveyed the scene, and nodded in satisfaction.

The lights went out, and the curtain fell.

Twenty-eight

Allie lay slumped on the stage in her death pose, her eyes closed, Michael's head in her lap. Over the sound of her heart, which was beating like a war drum, she listened for a reaction from the audience. There wasn't a whisper of sound in the huge theater, just a stunned silence. *It was a disaster,* she thought.

"Allie?" Michael whispered. "What happens now?"

"I don't know, Mikey," she answered shakily. Now that it was over, she felt frightened. She had no idea what might happen next.

Then Michael said, "Allie, look."

She opened her eyes and saw the spectral form of Skayendady hovering over them. Her face, no longer streaked with soot and tears, appeared serene.

"She's happy now," Michael said, sounding happy himself.

"Yes," Allie said. "I think she is."

Skayendady's lips moved, and Allie made out the word she spoke: *"Skennon."* Peace.

As the vision slowly blurred and faded, Allie thought, *Whatever happens next, it was worth it.*

The silence from the other side of the curtain was broken by a soft shuffling. Puzzled, Allie lifted her head and listened intently. Strangely, it sounded to her like many people moving about with muffled footsteps. She heard the wail of a siren growing louder, then stopping.

Miss Lunsford rushed onto the stage, where the massacre victims lay sprawled in mock death. Her face glowed. "Bravo, everyone! Bravo!"

"But," said Allie, feeling confused. "The audience—they're so quiet. Did they—?"

Miss Lunsford interrupted her to say excitedly, "Just wait. I was watching their faces. They need a minute to take it all in, to sort out their emotions." She paused, then smiled, saying, "There. Listen."

Someone had begun to clap. Then others joined in and the applause quickly built until the walls of the huge old opera house resounded with a thunderous roar.

"Get up, everyone!" Miss Lunsford urged. "Get ready for your curtain call!"

Allie and Michael stood, joining the rest of the cast, who were trying to form themselves into a long line so they could take a group bow. Allie held on to

Michael's hand and reached out her other hand to Dub. But Janelle came over, stood beside her, and grasped her hand instead.

Allie squeezed Janelle's hand and whispered, "Thank you."

Dub, seeing Janelle and Allie standing together, smiled and took Michael's other hand, and Brad, Joey, Pam, and Julie filled in beside him. Soon the entire cast was ready.

The curtain rose, and they all gasped in amazement. The applause was deafening. The crowd was on its feet. The houselights came on and, to Allie's surprise, the first person she saw was Ronnie, standing right in the front. She was dressed in traditional Seneca finery, and was looking directly at Allie with tears in her eyes. Her smile was almost fierce.

Standing with her, filling both aisles, were other people from the Seneca nation, many of them also wearing their traditional garb, clapping with grave dignity. Seeing the moccasins on Ronnie's feet, Allie understood the source of the quiet, shuffling steps she had heard. It had been Ronnie and her friends, stepping out of their seats to come forward.

Then she saw her mother and father, Dub's parents, and Mr. Henry, all gazing at the stage, clapping along with the rest of the crowd. Out of the corner of her eye she caught a glimpse of Karen Laver, the only person who remained seated, her arms crossed over her chest, her mouth shut in a tight line, her eyes narrowed in disgust.

Some people never change, Allie thought ruefully. She looked away. She wasn't going to let Karen ruin this moment for her. Instead she smiled at Janelle, whose face was shining with pride and pleasure.

Some of the cast members called for Miss Lunsford and Uncle Hal to come out and take a bow. They did, standing with Allie and the others on the stage, and still the crowd kept clapping.

Allie didn't know how long the applause might have gone on if an emergency medical crew hadn't come running to the front of the theater, wanting to know who was injured.

Twenty-nine

After several moments of confusion, Uncle Hal took charge. He led the ambulance crew to the little room backstage where Mr. Kavanaugh lay. Then he joined Allie, a grin of amusement on his face.

"He's going to be okay, right?" Allie asked.

Uncle Hal snorted. "I told you he's a hardhead. Right now he's back there giving everybody else a headache."

"Uncle Hal?" said Allie. "You said you had something in the van to keep Mr. Kavanaugh from making trouble if he woke up. What was it?"

Uncle Hal smiled and said solemnly, "Uncle Hal never reveals his secret methods, remember?"

Mr. and Mrs. Nichols came up onto the stage, and Allie saw that her mother's eyes and nose were red from crying. She wrapped Michael in one arm and Allie in the other and squeezed them tight, saying,

"That was incredible. I felt every bullet in my own heart."

Mr. Nichols leaned over to hug Allie, then Michael. "Did you two have to do such a good job of dying?" he asked. "I almost couldn't watch!" To Dub he said, "And your final speech was beautiful."

Other kids' parents gathered around, too, their expressions proud but sober. Miss Lunsford walked up then and joined the circle around Allie and Dub. "Well," she said, "it's been quite a night, hasn't it?"

Allie nodded, and glanced at Dub. He looked dazed, but relieved and happy, which was just how she felt.

There was no mistaking the mischievous gleam in Miss Lunsford's eyes as she continued. "Talk about improvising! That was spectacular." Turning to Uncle Hal, she stood on her tiptoes and, to Allie's delight, kissed him on the cheek. "And *you* were fantastic," she said softly.

Uncle Hal grinned, looking as if he had just broken five cinder blocks with his bare hands.

Mr. Henry stepped up then. "*That's* the way history should be taught," he declared. "This isn't a pretty story, but it's one that needs to be told. You made it come alive." In a whisper he added, "Later, when the dust settles, I hope you'll tell me what really happened here tonight."

"We will," Allie promised. She felt a hand on

her shoulder and turned around. "Ronnie!" she exclaimed happily. "I'm so glad you came!"

"After you told me about the pageant, I knew I had to come and see it for myself," Ronnie said. "As you see, I brought a good part of the Seneca nation with me!" Her face grew serious. "I was afraid of what we would see, that the pageant would be, as Skayendady said, a lie. But after what happened here tonight, I know she is pleased, as I am."

Allie nodded. "She is. She told me, '*Skennon.*'"

Ronnie smiled. "Yes. I feel this, too. Thank you."

Allie didn't answer, not knowing how to begin to thank Ronnie.

"I have hope that now, because of you, Poplar Point will remain as it is," she said quietly. "It is sacred ground, where my ancestors wish to rest in peace."

Allie nodded and said, "I hope so, too."

"Oh, I think you can count on that," someone said.

Allie, Dub, and Ronnie all looked up in surprise to see that Janelle and her mother had joined them. It was Mrs. Kavanaugh who had spoken.

"Congratulations, Allie and Dub, on your improvements to my script," she continued. "I mean that. I admire what you did here tonight."

We had a little help from a ghost, Allie thought.

And Uncle Hal, Miss Lunsford, and the other kids, including Janelle.

"I don't know how you managed it," Mrs. Kavanaugh went on. "It's not easy to stand up to Darryl. I know that all too well. But you've proven it can be done. And I promise you that my husband won't be building out at Poplar Point."

"But how can you stop him?" Allie couldn't help asking. She remembered Janelle saying, "You don't know my father. When he decides something, it happens."

Mrs. Kavanaugh gave a small, rueful smile. "He lost a lot of support here tonight. But it's not only that," she added firmly. "The project was backed with my money, and I am withdrawing it." She paused to put her arm around Janelle. "You—and my daughter—taught me a little something tonight about standing up for what is right."

Michael ran up then, his cheeks flushed deep red with excitement. He tugged on Allie's arm and said, "Come on! We're going to our house and ordering pizza and Miss Lunsford and Uncle Hal are coming and he's bringing all the smoke bombs he didn't use and Dad says we can set them off in the yard!" He tugged again. "Come *on*. Brad asked if Uncle Hal would break a board with his hand and he said yes!"

"Okay, okay, Mike," Allie said with a laugh. "Ronnie, can you come? And your friends?"

"*Hurry!*" Michael urged before running off.

Ronnie smiled. "Go," she said. "We'll see each other again." She touched her heart. "I feel it here."

Allie nodded and touched her own heart. Then she turned to Janelle and said, "Can you and your mom come?" She flushed and, not wanting to be rude, added quickly, "Your dad, too. If he wants."

Janelle didn't know that less than an hour earlier, very close to where they now stood talking, her father had grabbed Allie and threatened her. Allie had no intention of telling her, and she'd make sure Michael didn't, either. What mattered was that, because of Janelle's courage, things were going to be a little different in the Kavanaugh household from now on. What mattered was that Allie had a feeling she and Janelle could become friends. What mattered was that Poplar Point was going to remain as it was.

And Skayendady would be able to rest in peace.

Mrs. Kavanaugh said to Janelle, "Honey, I'm going to go to the hospital with your dad. The EMT is sure he's fine, but he has to get thoroughly checked out. There's no reason you can't go with Allie and Dub, though."

"Okay," Janelle said happily.

Michael was at Allie's side again, nearly breathless with excitement. "Allie, Dub, look! Uncle Hal said I could play with these, just for tonight, in case any more bad guys come!"

He held up his hands, handcuffed together. The cuffs looked sturdy and real, although they hung so loosely on Michael's little wrists that he could pull his hands out any time he wanted. For the moment, he was clearly enjoying the thrill of being "cuffed."

Allie's hand flew to her mouth as her mind formed a mental image of Darryl Kavanaugh handcuffed to the risers backstage while she and the cast carried out the final scene. Turning to Dub, she said, "You don't think . . . ?"

They looked at each other, wide-eyed.

Dub grinned and said, "Actually, yeah. I do. We're talking about Uncle Hal here, remember." He shrugged and added, "We may never know for sure, though. I don't think Mr. Kavanaugh's going to be going around telling the story!"

Allie added, "And Uncle Hal—"

Dub chimed in and, laughing, they finished together, *"never reveals his secret methods!"*

Author's Note

I live in central New York State, originally the territory of the Six Nations of Native Americans (Mohawk, Oneida, Onondaga, Cayuga, Seneca, and Tuscarora) that formed the Haudenosaunee, or Iroquois, Confederacy. My house sits on the shore of Seneca Lake, at Kashong Point. Seneca is the largest of the Finger Lakes and was named after the Seneca people, the first to hunt, fish, farm, and live here.

On the highway, just a few hundred yards from my house, stands a monument showing a map. It commemorates the 1779 campaigns of General John Sullivan and General James Clinton "against the hostile Indian nations" on the frontiers of New York and Pennsylvania.

Kashong Point once held a thriving Seneca village, with orchards and fields and large stores of grain, fruits, and vegetables. Now the area is a community park for lakeside homeowners. Except for a small sign that says simply SITE OF A SENECA INDIAN VILLAGE UNTIL 1779, there is no indication of the drama that occurred here on a warm September day in that year.

When I stand alone at the Point, looking at the swings, the ball diamond, and the pavilion where we have neighborhood dinners and celebrations, I try to picture the village before it was destroyed by Sullivan's army in a surprise massacre. I try to feel the presence of those Seneca Indians who lived and died here, and sometimes I can. Hence this book.

The story is fictional, but based on historical fact. The words spoken in the pageant by Dub (as Cornplanter, the famous Seneca orator), Joey (as General John Sullivan), and Brad (as General George Washington) are taken in large part from their letters and written accounts of their speeches. These may be found online at *www.sullivanclinton.com*, at *http:// earlyamerica.com/review/1998/sullivan.html*, and in John McIntosh's book *The History of the North American Indians* (partial title), published in 1859 and accessible through Google.